EnglishSmart in 90 Days 1

Mary Martin

Printed in China

Contents

EnglishSmart in 90 Days

GRADE 1

Birthday Surprise

Billy is six years old today. Mom and Dad have a special surprise for him. When he comes downstairs, Billy sees a cute little kitten. He runs over and picks up his new pet. It is small and round and white. "I think its name should be Snowball," said Billy.

Happy Birthday to Billy!
From Mom & Dad

A. Put the events in order by writing the letters in the  .

A Billy sees the kitten.

B Billy picks up his pet.

C Billy comes downstairs.

D Billy names it Snowball.

E Billy runs over to the kitten.

B. Fill in the blanks with words from the story.

1. Billy is _____ years old today.

2. The surprise is a little _____ .

3. The colour of the pet is _____ .

4. The name of the kitten will be _____ .

C. Match each cat with a good name.

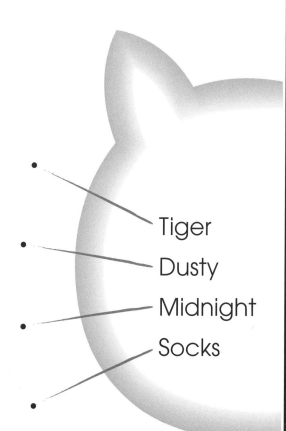

1. A black cat •   •

2. An orange cat •   •   Tiger

    Dusty

    Midnight

3. A grey cat •   •   Socks

4. A cat with white paws •   •

Did You Know?

Cats sleep 16 to 18 hours a day. How many hours do you sleep a day?

Day
2

Beginning Consonants (1)

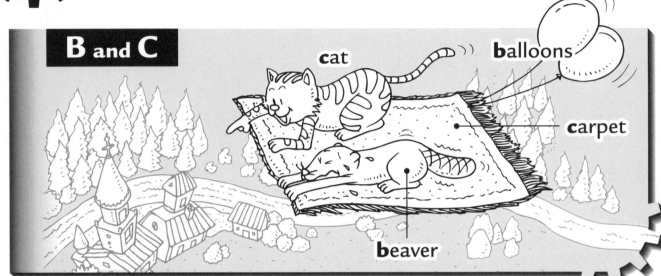

B and C

cat

balloons

carpet

beaver

A. Print the letter "Bb".

Bb

B. Say the things. Circle ○ the pictures that begin with the "b" sound.

C. Print the letter "Cc".

D. Say the things. Draw lines to join the pictures that begin with the "c" sound to the cake.

E. Draw one thing that begins with the "b" sound and another thing that begins with the "c" sound. Say the things.

A Thank You Letter

Dear Aunt Caroline,

Thank you for the book of zoo animals you sent for my birthday. I love the colourful pictures and I can read the information too. My favourite pages are about the monkeys. There are some funny pictures and also some cute baby monkeys.

I am going to take the book to school for my animal project. I will show you my project when you come to visit. Thanks again.

Love,
Cara

A. Fill in the blanks with words from the letter.

1. Cara got a _____ for her birthday.

2. It is about zoo _____ .

3. She likes the _____ best.

4. Cara will do a _____ on animals.

B. **Choose the correct sentence for each picture and write it on the lines.**

1. The monkey is asleep.
   The monkey went away.
   The monkey is eating.

   _____

   _____

2. The monkeys are in the jungle.
   The monkeys are in a cage.
   The monkeys are in a tree.

   _____

   _____

3. The book is about school.
   The book is about birthdays.
   The book is about animals.

   _____

   _____

Did You Know?

The Tarsier is the smallest monkey in the world. It is about the size of a rat. It can fit in the palm of your hand!

Beginning Consonants (2)

D and F

fox

dog

fence

dig

A. **Print the letter "Dd".**

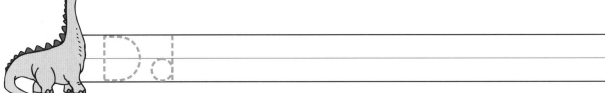

B. **Say the things. Print "d" for the pictures that begin with the "d" sound.**

1.

2.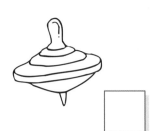

3.

4.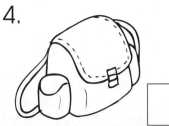

5.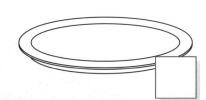

6.

C. Print the letter "Ff".

D. Say each pair of things. Cross out ✗ the one that does not begin with the "f" sound.

1.

2.

3.

4.

E. Say the things. Circle ◯ the correct beginning sound.

1.

d	f

2.

d	f

3.

d	f

Date : _____

Toast with Honey

Toast with honey,
Toast with jam,
Peanut butter,
Cheese, or ham.

Toast for breakfast,
Lunch or dinner,
I love toast,
It's just a winner!

A.   Choose the correct word ending to finish the "toast" words.

1.   I put the bagel in the toast_____ .

2.   Mom toast_____ two slices of bread.

3.   We like toast_____ marshmallows on the campfire.

B. **Unscramble the words to find out what the children like to have on their toast.**

1. Andrew likes to eat toast with (nohey) _____ .

2. Celia likes to eat toast with (maj) _____ .

3. Erica likes to eat toast with (seeche) _____ .

4. Alison likes to eat toast with (tterub) _____ .

5. Ian likes to eat toast with

 (mah) _____ .

C. **Finish the rhymes with words on the toast.**

1. Mom gave me some money,

 To go and buy _____ .

2. My friend's name is Sam.

 He likes strawberry _____ .

3. I have toast to munch,

 When it's time for _____ .

4. The thing I love most,

 Is honey on

 _____ .

lunch
honey
toast
jam

Did You Know?

In ancient times, bread was toasted over a fire or on a hot stone. In the early 1900s, the first toasters were produced.

Date : _____

Day
6

Beginning Consonants (3)

G and H

hippo   girl   ghost   house

A.   Print the letter "Gg".

B.   Say the things on the path. Help Gordon the Goose get to the garden by circling ◯ the pictures that begin with the "g" sound.

C. Print the letter "Hh".

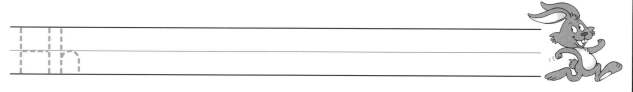

D. Say the things. Colour the ♡ for the pictures that begin with the "h" sound.

1.  ♡

2. ♡

3.  ♡

4.  ♡

5.  ♡

E. Say the things. Print "g" for the pictures that begin with the "g" sound. Print "h" for those that begin with the "h" sound.

1.

☐

2.

☐

3.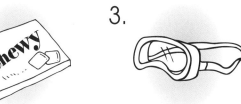

☐

4.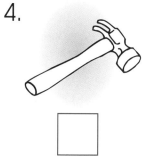

☐

How Honey Is Made

A honeybee is an insect that collects nectar from flowers and uses it to make honey. A beehive is a structure where bees can build a honeycomb.

The honeycomb has rows of six-sided cells where the bees store honey. When it is ready, the beekeeper collects the honey and we can use it for a sweet treat!

A. Join the word and picture to write a word.

1. honey   +   =   _____

2. [bee picture]   +   hive   =   _____

B. Choose the correct word to complete the sentence.

flowers   insect   six   sweet

1. A honeybee is an _____ .

2. Bees collect nectar from _____ .

3. The cells in a honeycomb have _____ sides.

4. The taste of honey is _____ .

C. Choose the correct word to finish each rhyme.

honey
bee
beehive
honeycomb

1. What do I see?

   I think it's a _____ .

2. Bees make their home,

   In a big _____ .

3. When the weather is sunny,

   The bees will make _____ .

4. They soon will arrive,

   At their special

   _____ .

Did You Know?

A bee has to visit over 2,000 flowers to produce just one pound of honey.

Beginning Consonants (4)

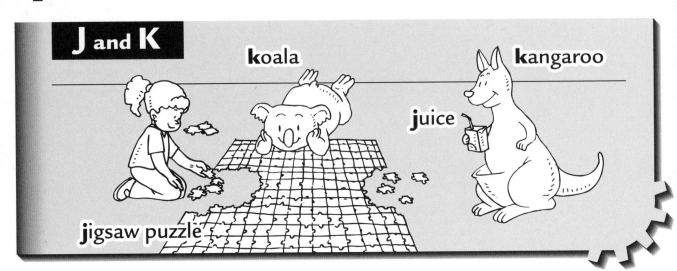

J and K

koala   kangaroo

juice

jigsaw puzzle

A.   Print the letter "Jj".

**B.   Say the things. Draw lines to join the pictures that begin with the "j"
        sound to the jack-o'-lantern.**

C. Print the letter "Kk".

K

D. Say the things. Colour the pictures that begin with the "k" sound.

E. Say the things. Write the missing beginning letters of the words.

1.

___acket

2.

___ettle

3.

___itchen

4.

___eep

5.

___ellyfish

6.

___ayak

Number Rhymes

Read this famous number rhyme.

One, two, buckle my shoe.
Three, four, shut the door.
Five, six, pick up sticks.
Seven, eight, lay them straight.
Nine, ten, a big fat hen.

A. Add the missing number words to make a new number rhyme.

One, 1._____ , stick with glue.

Three, 2._____ , go to the store.

Five, 3._____ , build with bricks.

Seven, 4._____ , open the gate.

Nine, 5._____ , write with a pen.

B. Use number words to complete each sentence.

1. Ben likes the story of Snow White and the _____ Dwarfs.

2. Cara likes the story of the _____ Little Pigs.

3. We have _____ fingers on each hand.

4. We have _____ toes on each foot.

5. When _____ babies are born at the same time, they are twins.

6. When _____ babies are born at the same time, they are triplets.

7. There are _____ quarters in a dollar.

8. There are _____ seasons in a year.

9. There are _____ days in a week.

10. There are _____ months in a year.

11. There are _____ wheels on a bicycle.

12. There are _____ wheels on a tricycle.

You Deserve A Break!

Match the words with the pictures by colouring each pair the same colour. Use a different colour for each pair.

bagels

balloons

bananas

basket

beans

boots

bow

bunny

bus

Beginning Consonants (5)

L and M

magnifying glass

monster

lightning

lamp

A. Print the letter "Ll".

B. Say the things. Cross out ✗ the pictures that do not begin with the "l" sound.

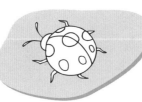

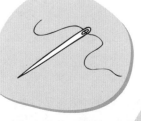

C. Print the letter "Mm".

M m

D. Say the things. Write "m" for the pictures that begin with the "m" sound.

E. Say the things. Write the letters for the pictures that begin with the "l" sound on the leaf. Write the letters for those that begin with the "m" sound on the mug.

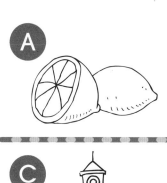

A

B

C

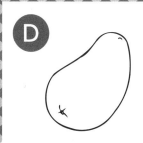

D

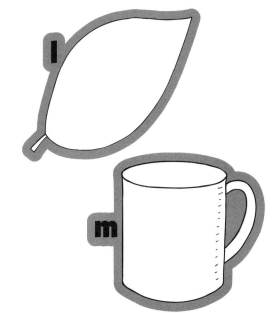

l

m

Date : _____

Day
12

The Three Little Pigs

You have probably heard the famous story of The Three Little Pigs. The story below tells the main ideas of the story.

Once upon a time there were three little pigs. The first pig made a house of straw but the wolf blew the house down. The second pig made a house of wood but the wolf blew the house down. The third pig made a house of bricks.

The wolf could not blow it down so he climbed down the chimney. But the third little pig was clever. He put a pot of hot water in the fireplace to trap the wolf.

A. Write "Yes" if the sentence is true. Write "No" if the sentence is not true.

1. The first pig made a house of wood.   _____

2. The wolf climbed down the chimney
    of the wood house.   _____

3. The third pig was very smart.   _____

4. The brick house was the strongest.   _____

B. **Look at each picture and choose the sentence that tells about the picture. Write the sentence on the lines.**

The wolf blew down the house of straw.
The wolf blew down the house of wood.
The wolf climbed down the chimney.
The wolf fell into a pot of hot water.

1.

_____

_____

2.

_____

_____

3.

_____

_____

4.

_____

_____

Day **13**

Beginning Consonants (6)

N and P

necklace

parachute

nest

pig

A. Print the letter "Nn".

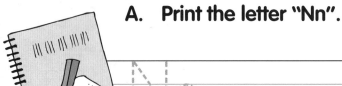

Nn

B. Say the things. Colour the pictures that begin with the "n" sound.

C. Print the letter "Pp".

P p

D. Say the things. Unscramble the words and write them on the lines. Check ✔ the pictures that begin with the "p" sound.

1. roprta ◯

2. acep ◯

3. picl ◯

4. nipao ◯

E. Say the things. Draw lines to join the pictures that begin with the "n" sound to the nest and those that begin with the "p" sound to the pizza.

 n

 p

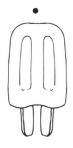    9

Kim's Rainbow

Kim got a new pack of crayons at the dollar store. She drew a picture of a rainbow. She used all the rainbow colours. There were red and orange and yellow and green and blue and purple too. She even drew a big yellow sun and some sparkly raindrops.

Mom was very proud of Kim's picture so she put it up on the fridge. Everyone loved Kim's colourful rainbow.

A. Read the colour words and use your crayons to colour the rainbow.

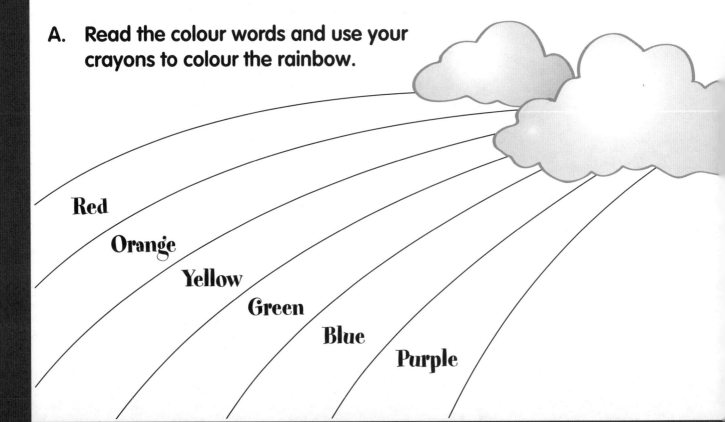

Red

Orange

Yellow

Green

Blue

Purple

B. Unscramble the colour word in each sentence. Colour the picture.

1. The apple is (der).

    _____

2. The pumpkin is (roaneg).

    _____

3. The sun is (llowye).

    _____

4. The frog is (neerg).

    _____

5. The jeans are (leub).

    _____

6. The plum is (plepur).

    _____

Beginning Consonants (7)

Q and R

Quiet, please.

quill

rooster

rabbit

A. Print the letter "Qq".

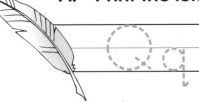

B. Say the things. Circle ◯ the picture that begins with the "q" sound in each group.

1.

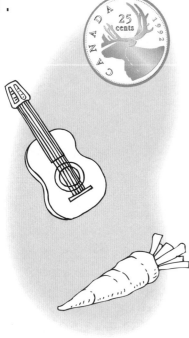

2.

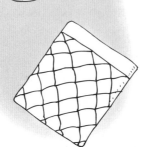

3.

C. Print the letter "Rr".

D. Circle ◯ four things that begin with the "r" sound in the picture. Say the things. Write their names on the lines.

_____

_____

_____

_____

E. Say the things. Write the beginning letters to complete the words. Then draw lines to join the words to the correct pictures.

1.  •

• ☐ hino

2. 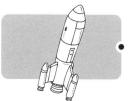 •

• ☐ uack

3.  •

• ☐ ueen

4.  •

• ☐ ocket

Mixing Colours

Have you ever tried to mix two colours together? You can mix paints, food colouring, or crayons. You will find that you can make some different colours. It seems like magic but it is really science!

There are three primary colours. These are red, yellow, and blue. You can mix red, blue, and yellow to make orange, green, and purple.

A. Colour the shapes using only your red, yellow, and blue crayons.

1.

(red) + (yellow) = (   )

2.

(blue) + (yellow) = (   )

3.

(red) + (blue) = (   )

Did you know that you can get the colour black by mixing together all the other colours? You can try this on some drawing paper. Use paints or crayons.

Black is the colour of a dark night. It is the colour of coal or wood that has burned. We think of black at Halloween when we see witches, bats, and black cats.

B. Use the word "black" to complete the story. Draw a picture to go with it.

Olga the Witch is wearing

a 1._____ hat and a

2._____ cape. She

has two pets. They are

a bat and a 3._____

cat. One day Olga noticed

a bad smell. There was a

4._____ and white

skunk in her backyard!

Date : _____

Day 17

Beginning Consonants (8)

S and T

Santa Claus

sign

town

Angel Town

toboggan

A. Print the letter "Ss".

Ss

B. Say the things. Draw the pictures that begin with the "s" sound in the sock.

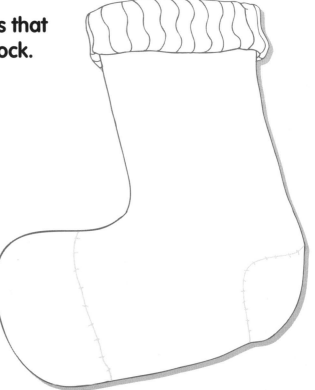

C. Print the letter "Tt".

T   T

D. Say the things. Check ✔ the pictures that begin with the "t" sound.

1.  ☐

2. ☐

3. ☐

4. ☐

E. Say the things in the picture. Colour those that begin with the "s" sound blue. Colour those that begin with the "t" sound yellow.

Date : _____

Breakfast Menu

Ben and Cara are staying at a hotel in Florida. In the morning they have a special breakfast menu for kids. Read the choices on the menu.

Happy Elephant RESTAURANT

Kid's Breakfast Menu

Breakfast 1
- Apple juice
- Waffles
- Ham
- Yogurt

Breakfast 2
- Pancakes
- Sausage
- Milk
- Banana

Breakfast 3
- Bagel
- Cream cheese
- Cranberry juice

Breakfast 4
- Orange juice
- Toast
- Bacon

Only $3.99 each

Read the items on the menu. Place each item in the correct food group.

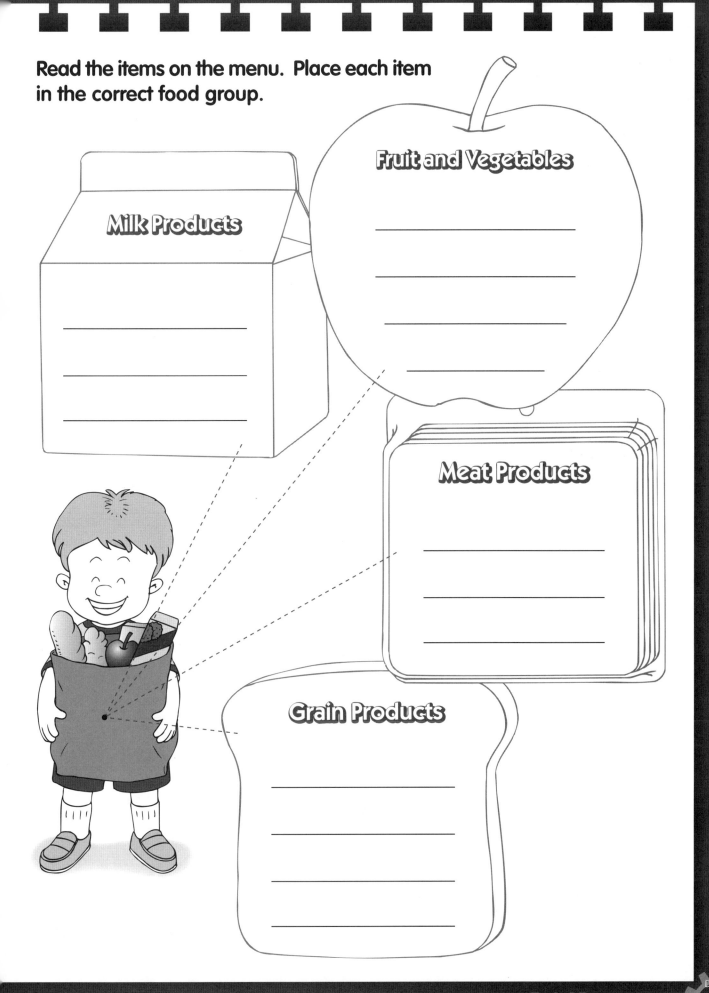

Fruit and Vegetables

Milk Products

Meat Products

Grain Products

Beginning Consonants (9)

A. Print the letter "Vv".

B. Say the things. Draw lines to join the pictures that begin with the "v" sound to the letter "v".

V .

C. Print the letter "Ww".

W w

D. Say the things. Complete the words for the pictures that begin with the "w" sound.

1.

___histle

2.

___ridge

3.

___atermelon

4.

___obot

5.

___indmill

6.

___allet

E. Say the things. Colour [v] for the pictures that begin with the "v" sound. Colour [w] for the pictures that begin with the "w" sound.

1.

V	W

2.

V	W

3.

V	W

4.

V	W

You Deserve A Break!

Put the words in alphabetical order on the lines. Then colour the ⬭
that contain animal words.

airplane

monkey

hippo

lemon

1. _____   2. _____

3. _____   4. _____

5. _____   6. _____

7. _____   8. _____

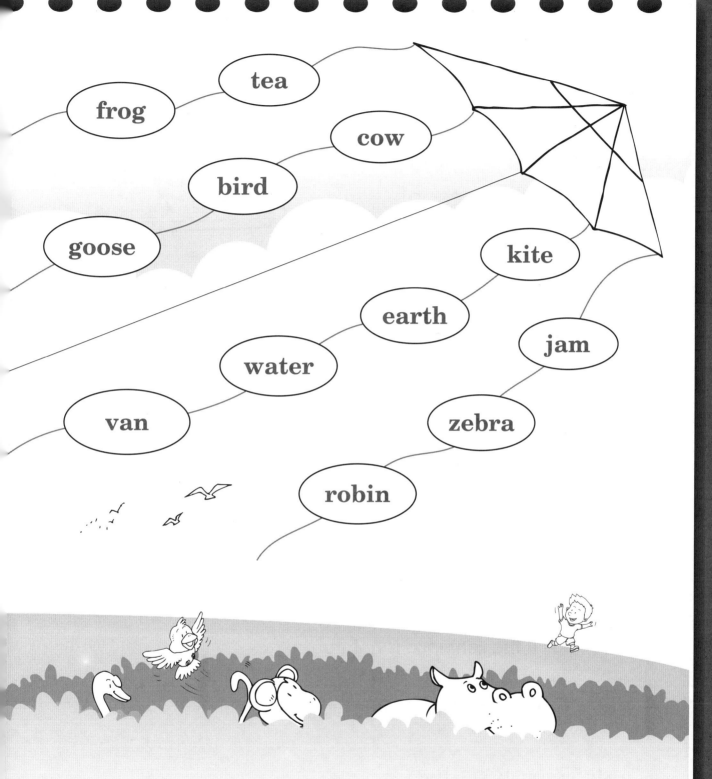

frog

tea

cow

bird

goose

kite

earth

jam

water

van

zebra

robin

9. _____

10. _____

11. _____

12. _____

13. _____

14. _____

15. _____

16. _____

Date : _____

Day **21**

Lunch at School

- apple
- ba~~n~~nna

It is the first day of grade one and Justin is very excited. He is going to stay at school all day. Mom packed a special lunch with his favourite food. She gave him a cheese sandwich, a banana, apple juice, and some treats. Justin thinks that the best thing about grade one is eating lunch at school!

A. **Write "Yes" if the sentence is true.**
   Write "No" if the sentence is not true.

1. Justin has a banana for lunch.

2. Justin is in grade two.

3. Justin likes eating lunch at school.

4. Dad made lunch for Justin.

B. Read the words in each group. Three things belong in the same group. One thing does not belong. Cross out ✗ the word that does not belong.

1.
apple
banana
peach
fish

2.
milk
juice
school
water

3.
one
hello
two
three

4.
lunch
dinner
breakfast
today

C. Fill in the missing letters to spell the words. Each word is missing the same two letters.

1. Justin had lun_____ at s_____ool today.

2. He likes to eat _____eese.

3. The boy is eating a sandwi_____ .

4. Do you want a banana or a pea_____ ?

5. Ea_____ girl has an apple.

Day
22

Beginning Consonants (10)

X, Y, and Z

yawn
yak
zebra
x-ray

A. Print the letters "Xx" and "Yy".

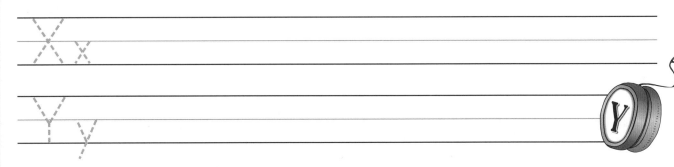

B. Say the things. Colour the pictures that begin with the "x" sound green. Colour those that begin with the "y" sound pink.

C. Print the letter "Zz".

D. Fill in the missing beginning letters. Say the words. Draw lines to match them with the pictures.

 ero

 oo

 ig-zag

 ucchini

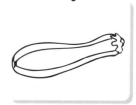

E. Say the things. Unscramble the words and write them on the lines. Circle ◯ the beginning letters.

1.

omzo

2.

rgtyuo

3.

kylo

4.

ipezpr

1. _____

2. _____

3. _____

4. _____

Polar Bears at the Zoo

On Sunday we went to the zoo. My favourite place was the polar bear pool. The polar bears like to cool off in the cold water. We watched them dive and swim and play together.

There is a special viewing area where we can look through a big window and see them swim underwater. It was exciting to watch them diving for fish at feeding time!

A. Fill in the blanks.

window   fish
   pool   zoo

1. There are polar bears at the _____ .

2. The polar bears swim in a _____ .

3. The polar bears like to eat _____ .

4. We looked through a _____ to watch the polar bears.

B. Match the zoo animal with the food it eats.

1. Monkey •
2. Lion •
3. Penguin •
4. Giraffe •

C. Match the zoo animal with the way it can move.

1.  2.  3.  4.

•   •   •   •

•   •   •   •

fly   swim   hop   run

D. Write one more animal you can see at the zoo. Draw a picture of the animal.

_____

Day
24

Ending Consonants (1)

B, C, D, and F

picnic

dad

cub

leaf

A. Say the things. Colour the pictures with the correct ending sounds.

1.

c

2.

d

3.

f

4.

d

5.

b

6.

b

7.

b

B. Say the things. Draw lines to join the pictures to the ending consonants on the balloons.

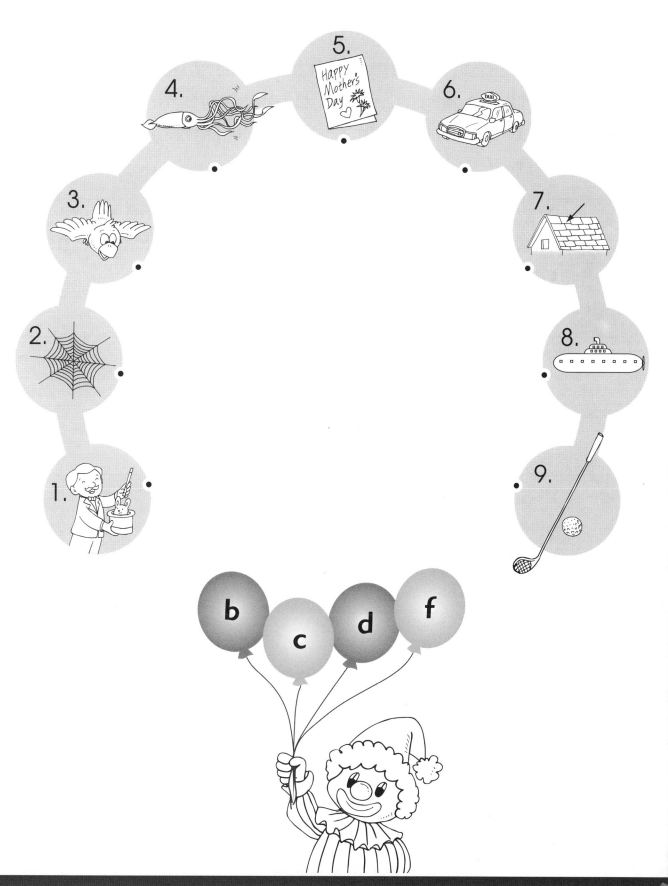

Arctic Polar Bears

Polar bears live in the Arctic where it is very cold. They have thick, white fur which looks very beautiful and also keeps them warm. Polar bears have large paws for walking on the ice. They also use their paws to help them swim underwater.

Polar bears are expert hunters and have good eyesight, excellent hearing, and a keen sense of smell. Arctic polar bears often travel long distances in search of food.

A. Choose another title for this page. Write it on the line.

Beautiful Polar Bears

Polar Bears Go Hunting

All About Polar Bears

The best title is _____.

B. Write "Yes" if the sentence is true. Write "No" if the sentence is not true.

1. Polar bears live in the Arctic. _____

2. Polar bears have big paws. _____

3. Polar bears can swim underwater. _____

4. Polar bears can't hear clearly. _____

5. Polar bears have a good sense of smell. _____

6. Polar bears are good hunters. _____

C. Unscramble the mixed up words and write the correct spelling.

1. Polar bears use their _____ to help them swim.

2. Polar bears live in the Arctic where the weather is very

_____ .

3. They have thick _____ fur.

4. The polar bears hunt

for _____ .

Did You Know?

When it is very very cold, polar bears dig a hole in the snow and ice to have a "winter sleep".

Day 26

Ending Consonants (2)

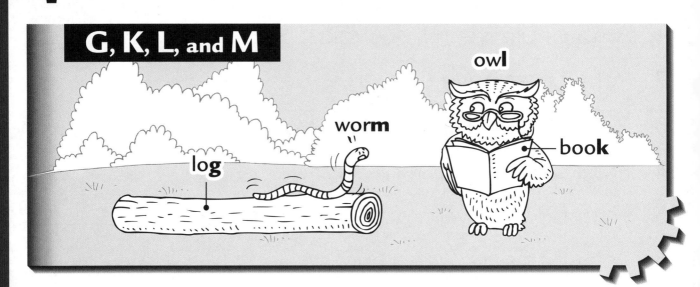

G, K, L, and M

owl

worm

log

book

A. Say the things. Circle ◯ the correct ending sounds of the words.

1.

| g | k | l | m |

2.

| g | k | l | m |

3.

| g | k | l | m |

4.

| g | k | l | m |

5.

| g | k | l | m |

6.

| g | k | l | m |

B. Say the things on the path. Help Greg get to school by writing the ending consonants of the words.

1.
2.
3.
4.
5.
6.
7.
8.
9.
10.
11.
12.
13.
14.
15.
16.
17.

Budgie Birds

Birds can be good pets. The most popular pet bird is the budgie. They are easy to look after and need only water and bird seed. They like to have ladders, bells, and mirrors in their cage. Budgies are fun to watch and they can even learn to talk. They can live for about six to ten years. Another name for a budgie is a parakeet.

A.   The words in brackets are mixed up. Write the sentences correctly.

1. Budgie birds (good   are   pets).

   _____

2. They (eat   to   like) bird seed.

   _____

3. The bird is (a   cage   in).

   _____

4. Budgie birds can (talk   to   learn).

   _____

B. Match the pet with its home.

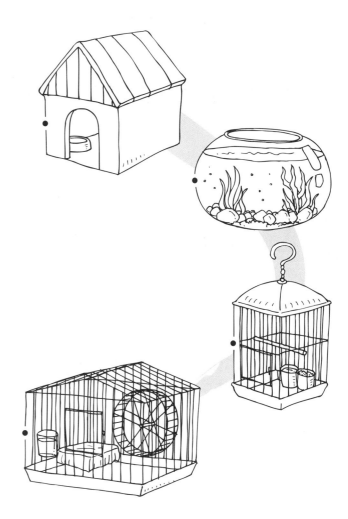

1. Bird   •

2. Dog   •

3. Goldfish •

4. Hamster •

C. Unscramble the action word for each pet.

1. I am a dog. I can (rabk) _____ .

2. I am a fish. I can (msiw) _____ .

3. I am a bird. I can (yfl) _____ .

4. I am a hamster. I can

    (nur) _____ .

Day
28

Ending Consonants (3)

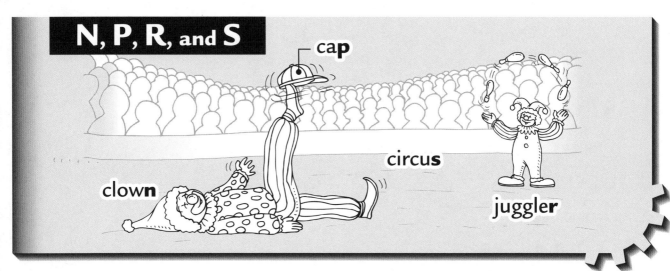

N, P, R, and S

cap

clown

circus

juggler

A. Say the things on the flowers. Complete the words with the correct ending consonants.

1. pea___

2. glas___

3. pi___

4. to___

5. cactu___

6. acor___

7. soa___

8. sta___

B. Say the things. Match the pictures with the words. Draw lines to join the first part of the words to the ending consonants.

• tige •	
• stam •	
• crow •	
• chai •	
• rhinocero •	
• snowma •	
• octopu •	
• iro •	
• spide •	
• shee •	

n
p
r
s

CANADA 50

Grandma's Pet

My grandma has a pet budgie bird named Pete. Pete is green with yellow and black stripes. She keeps him in a cage in the kitchen and he keeps her company while she is working.

Sometimes Grandma lets him out of his cage to fly around. If Pete is in a good mood, he says, "Have a nice day." I love it when he talks and I am happy that my grandma has such a friendly pet.

A. **Find three colour words in the story. Write one on each line. Then use it to colour the puff of cream.**

B. Use the words in the cage to fill in the blanks. Use each word only once.

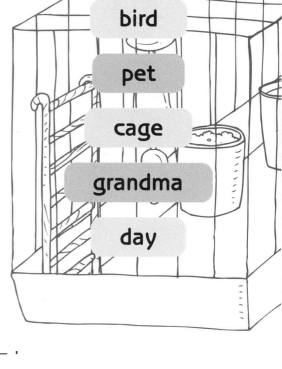

bird

pet

cage

grandma

day

1. The budgie _____ is colourful.

2. Pete can say, "Have a nice _____ ."

3. My _____ has a pet bird.

4. She keeps the bird in a _____ .

5. A bird is a good _____ .

C. Write "Yes" if the sentence is true. Write "No" if the sentence is not true.

1. The bird in the story is a boy. _____

2. Some birds can talk. _____

3. The bird is named Happy. _____

4. Grandma keeps the bird cage in the garden.

   _____

5. Grandma likes Pete.

   _____

Did You Know?

Some budgies like to roll around in wet lettuce leaves to clean themselves.

Day
30

You Deserve A
Break!

Fill in the missing letters below to find out what Katie is singing about.
Then write down what you see in the picture to get the whole song.

 h__pp__ f__c__

 r__bb__n

 m__rbl__s

 b__ __ds

 c__rn ch__ps

 l__m__n p__ __ls

1. On the first day of school my teacher sang to me,

   A r__bb__n around a h__pp__ f__c__ .

2. On the second day of school my teacher sang to me,

   Two pretty m__rbl__s, and

   A _____ around a _____ _____ .

3. 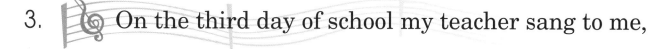 On the third day of school my teacher sang to me,

Three c___rn ch___ps,

Two _____ _____ , and

A _____ around a _____ _____ .

4. On the fourth day of school my teacher sang to me,

Four l___m___n p_____ls,

Three _____ _____ ,

Two _____ _____ , and

A _____ around a _____ _____ .

5. On the fifth day of school

 my teacher sang to me,

Five str___ngs ___f b_____ds!

Four _____ _____ ,

Three _____ _____ ,

Two _____ _____ , and

A _____ around a

_____ _____ !

Day 31

Ending Consonants (4)

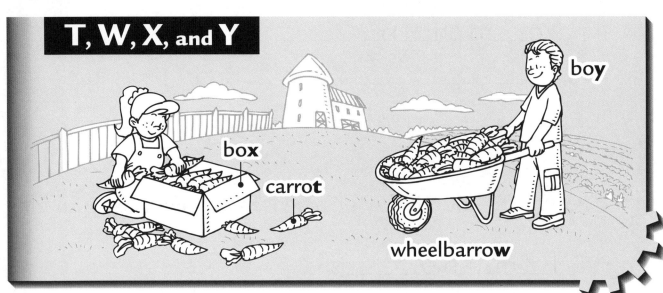

T, W, X, and Y

box

carrot

wheelbarrow

boy

A. Say the things. Colour the boxes with the correct ending consonants to complete the words.

1.

co | y | w

2.

turke | x | y

3.

puppe | y | t

4.

fo | t | x

5.

walnu | t | x

6.

si | x | y

7.

pillo | w | t

8.

monke | y | w

B. Say the things. Unscramble the words and write them in the boxes. Circle ◯ the ending consonants of the words.

1. 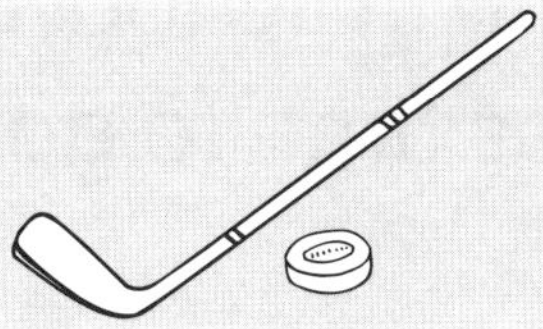 echkyo

2. 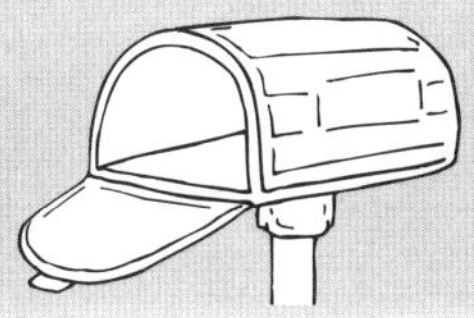 iaxbmol

3.  ptoaet

4.  iwronab

5.  aehtr

6. 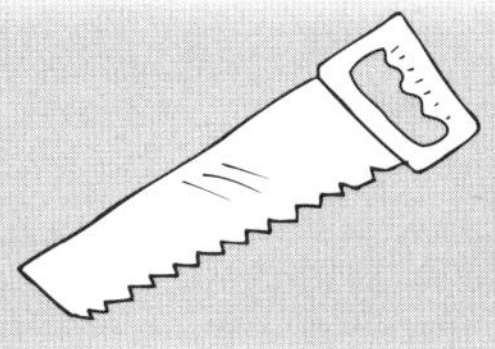 was

7. 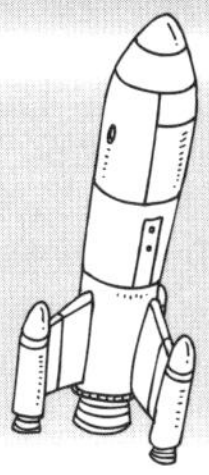 trecok

8.  tayr

Five Little Kittens

It was Steve's first day of school. He had fun at school and he met some new friends. At 12 o'clock it was time to go home for lunch. Steve ran up the front steps and into the kitchen. He was very hungry!

But instead of lunch, there was a big surprise in the kitchen. It was a basket with five little kittens. While he was at school, his cat had kittens. Steve was so excited! His first day of school had been a really special day.

A. Circle ◯ the correct word in each sentence.

1. It was the (first / last) day of school.

2. At 12 o'clock it was time for (school / lunch) .

3. He found the kittens in a (box / basket) .

4. There were (four / five) kittens.

5. Steve's family has a pet (cat / dog) .

B. Draw a line to match each mother animal with her baby.

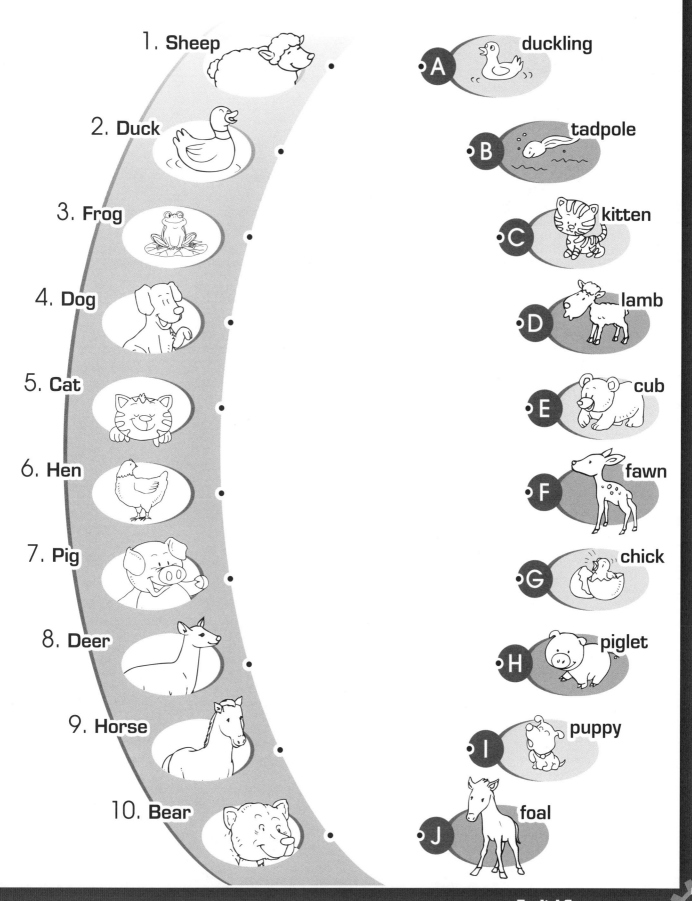

1. Sheep

2. Duck

3. Frog

4. Dog

5. Cat

6. Hen

7. Pig

8. Deer

9. Horse

10. Bear

A duckling

B tadpole

C kitten

D lamb

E cub

F fawn

G chick

H piglet

I puppy

J foal

Short Vowels (1)

A and E

hen

panda

cat

bell

A.   Print the letter "Aa".

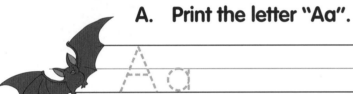

A a

B.   Say the things in each bag. Colour the one with the short "a" sound.

1

2

3

CANADA 50

C. Print the letter "Ee".

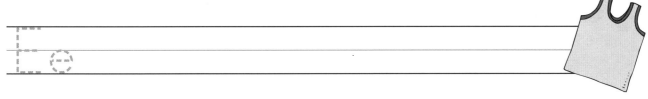

D. Say the things. Write the letter "e" to finish the words. Draw lines to join the words to the pictures.

 1

2

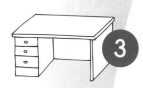 3

4

 5

6

 7

8

9

10

-    l__mon   •
-    h__lm__t   •
-    __gg   •
-    d__sk   •
-    p__nguin   •
-    sl__d   •
-    n__t   •
-    w__b   •
-    w__ll   •
-    t__nt   •

Show and Tell

Steve's teacher said he could bring his kitten to school for Show and Tell. His dad helped him practise some things to say. Here is Steve's speech:

"This is my kitten. He is two months old and his name is Bedford. When my cat had kittens, Bedford was my favourite because he is so white and fluffy. He likes water and special kitten food. His favourite toy is a wind-up mouse that he can chase.

When I get home from school every day, I like to cuddle Bedford and watch him play."

A. Find these words in Steve's speech.

1. A colour word: _____

2. A number word: _____

3. A drink: _____

4. Three animal words:

_____   _____   _____

B. Read what Steve's teacher says and write the words on the lines in each group.

Take a look at these words on the board. Can you sort them into groups?

red   five   cat   milk
blue   six   pig   juice
green   two   pop   three
mouse   horse   water   white

Colour   **Number**   **Animal**   **Drink**

_____   _____   _____   _____

_____   _____   _____   _____

_____   _____   _____   _____

_____   _____   _____   _____

Short Vowels (2)

I, O, and U

pig

mummy

robot

A.   Print the letter "Ii".

I

i

B.   Say the things. Circle ◯ the pictures with the short "i" sound. Find the words in the word search.

b	u	f	i	s	h	d
h	l	m	y	v	q	c
r	m	y	k	d	h	o
c	i	o	p	i	l	j
s	t	n	b	f	x	z
d	t	i	r	m	t	d
k	e	s	n	o	b	s
t	n	g	c	l	i	p
l	v	w	e	r	b	h

C. Print the letter "Oo".

D. Read the clue for each short "o" riddle. Write the word on the lines. Circle ◯ the short "o" of the word.

1. I wag my tail when I'm happy. __ __ __

2. I'm a toy that spins. __ __ __

3. I live in the ocean. I've eight long arms. __ __ __ __ __ __ __ __

4. I'm a cold treat on a stick. __ __ __ __ __ __ __ __ __

5. You can find lots of trees in me. __ __ __ __ __ __ __

E. Print the letter "Uu".

F. Say the words on the ducks. Colour the ducks with short "u" words.

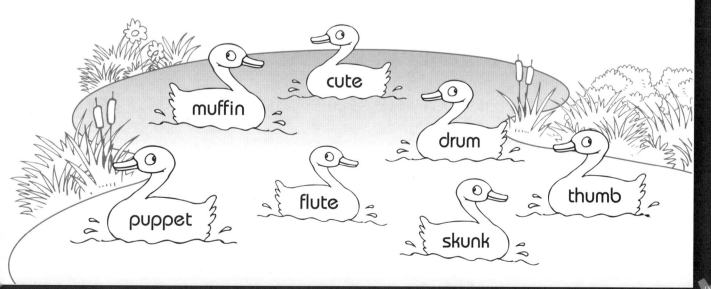

cute

muffin

drum

flute

puppet

skunk

thumb

Favourite Recipes

Here is a recipe for a healthy snack that is easy to make. It is called "Ants on a Log"!

What you need

- bunch of celery
- cream cheese
  - raisins

What to do

- Cut off celery leaves.
- Cut celery into long pieces.
- Spread cream cheese on each piece.
- Put a few raisins on top.

A. Fill in the blanks with words from the recipe.

First you get a bunch of 1._____ and cut off the leaves. Then cut the celery into pieces. Spread some cream 2._____ on each piece. Next add a few 3._____ on top. The raisins will look like 4._____ sitting on a log!

Here is a recipe for a sweet treat you can make using the microwave. It is called "S'Mores" because you will want "some more"!

What you need

graham crackers

squares of chocolate
(or chocolate chips)

mini marshmallows

What to do

- Take one graham cracker.

- Put a piece of chocolate on top.

- Add a mini marshmallow.

- Heat in the microwave for a few seconds until the chocolate and marshmallow melt.

B.   Fill in the blanks with words from the recipe.

First you get one graham 1._____ . Then you

put a small piece of 2._____ and a mini

3._____ on top. Heat in the microwave for a

few 4._____ . Enjoy eating the "S'Mores"!

Day 37

Short Vowels – Review

A. Say the words. Look at the highlighted letters and put the words in the correct columns. Colour the picture.

lamp   mug   pen   butterfly   kid   plant   letter
pot   window   cats   lollipop   lizard

Short "a" words	Short "e" words	Short "i" words	Short "o" words	Short "u" words
Colour them yellow.	Colour them pink.	Colour them blue.	Colour them red.	Colour them orange.

B. Say the things. The short vowels of the words under the pictures are wrong. Correct the words on the lines.

1.
bunch

_____

2.
dirt

_____

3.
watch

_____

4.
cord

_____

5.
bud

_____

6.
shop

_____

7.
pin

_____

8.
black

_____

9.
jog

_____

10.
click

_____

11.
battle

_____

12.
track

_____

Date : _____

Day **38**

Pancakes

Pancakes, pancakes,

Nothing tastes better.

Winter, summer,

Any kind of weather.

Milk, eggs, flour, butter,

Measure, mix, stir together.

Pour the batter in the pan.

Some for Sue and some for Dan.

Flip them over, soon they're done.

Some for Dad and some for Mom.

Everybody fills their plate.

Pancakes and syrup,

Taste so great!

A. Fill in the blanks with words from the passage.

1. Name four ingredients you need to make pancakes.

    _____   _____

    _____   _____

2. A word that means a mixture for
    baking   _____

3. Something sweet and sticky to go
    on pancakes   _____

4. A word that rhymes with "great"   _____

B. Cross out ✗ the word that does not belong in each group.

1   pasta   syrup   jam   honey

2   pancakes   candy   cereal   toast

3   Dan   Sue   Mandy   Canada

4   plate   dish   spoon   bowl

Long Vowels (1)

A, I, O, and U

piano

violin

music

stage

Long vowels sound the same as the way you say the letters.

A. Say the things in each group. Cross out ✘ the picture that does not have the long "a" sound.

1.

2.

3.

4.

B. Read the sentences aloud. Circle ◯ the long "i" words.

1. Can you find the rhino in the picture?

2. Linda is reading a book about dinosaurs in the library.

3. The price of the antique vase is really high.

4. The pirates hid the diamonds on the island.

5. The tiger is looking at the spider on the sign.

C. Say the things. Complete the puzzles with long "o" words.

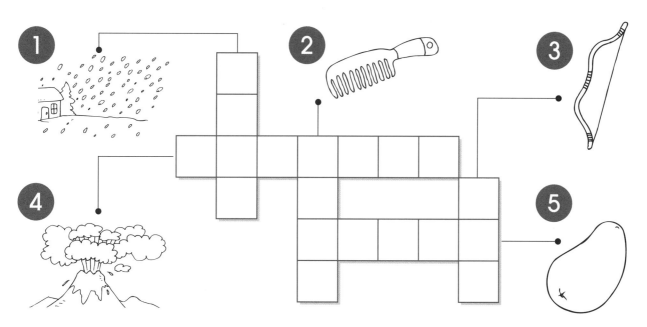

D. Say the things. Colour the pictures that have the long "u" sound.

Day 40

You Deserve A Break!

There are eight differences in these two pictures. Can you find them?
Use a different colour to colour each one.

Colour one magnifying
glass when you find
a difference.

Wendy the Witch

Wendy the Witch is a scary sight,
When she flies,
On Halloween night.

She has a green face and green teeth too,
Her hair is orange and purple and blue.

She wears a black cape and a big, black hat,
On her broomstick she carries an owl and a bat.

Wendy the Witch is a scary sight,
When she rides her broomstick,
On Halloween night.

A. Use an orange crayon to colour the rhyming words in each row of pumpkins.

1.  sight   laugh    night

2.  blue   too    grow

3.  what   hat    bat

B. Help Wendy the Witch get ready for Halloween night.

1. Give Wendy a black hat and a black cape.
2. Colour her face and teeth green.
3. Colour her hair orange, purple, and blue.
4. Draw an owl and a bat on her broomstick.

hat

cape

owl

bat

Did You Know?

The word "witch" comes from an old English word "wicce" which means "the wise one".

Long Vowels (2)

Long Vowels with Silent "E"

cake   mice   hole   flute

A. Fill in the blanks with the long-vowel words.

> dime   hate   huge
> note   pine   rode   tube

Add the silent "e" to one of the words in the sentence to form the long-vowel word.

1. Ginny gave the _____ teddy bear a big hug.

2. I _____ wearing the red hat.

3. Pin the _____ cone on the board.

4. Dad _____ to the shop to buy a fishing rod.

5. There is not a _____ in the book.

6. Don't leave the _____ of toothpaste in the tub.

7. He could not find the _____ in the dim light.

B. Say the things. Add long vowels and silent "e" to complete the words. Match the words with the pictures by writing the letters in the boxes.

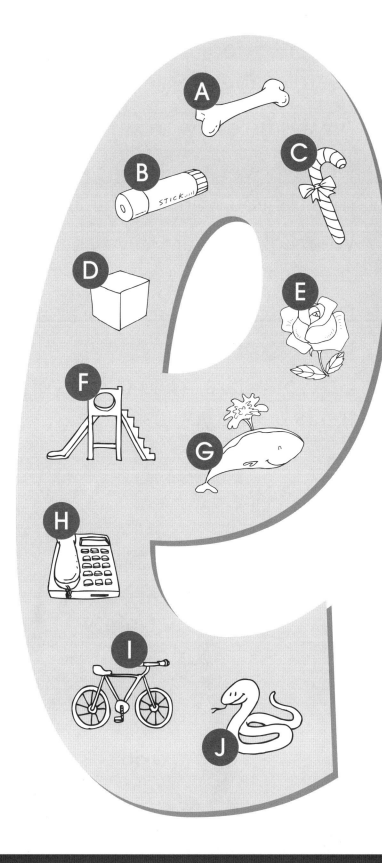

1. c___n___ ☐

2. gl___ ___ ☐

3. b___n___ ☐

4. sn___k___ ☐

5. ph___n___ ☐

6. b___k___ ☐

7. sl___d___ ☐

8. r___s___ ☐

9. wh___l___ ☐

10. c___b___ ☐

Day
43

Halloween Safety Rules

On Halloween night children like to go trick-or-treating. They dress up in costumes and go door to door collecting treats. At school the children learn these rules about Halloween Safety:

- Always go out with an adult.

- Don't cover your eyes with a mask or you won't be able to see.

- Wear light colours so you can be seen in the dark.

- Don't wear costumes that are too long or you might trip.

- Get your parents to check your treats before you eat them.

A. Use the words on the pumpkin to finish these rhymes.

1. Wear colours that are _____
   When you go out at night.

2. Don't run or jump or skip.
   Be careful or you'll _____ .

3. Be sure to check each _____
   Before you start to eat.

4. Don't be silly fools.
   Follow the safety _____ .

Halloween Safety

light
treat
trip
rules

B. Wendy the Witch did a "Backward Spell" on some words. Change them around so they are correct.

1. Nadim wore a curly wig with his

    (nwolc) _____ costume.

2. Mai wore a silver crown with her

    (ssecnirp) _____ costume.

3. Jenny wore a pointed hat with her

    (hctiw) _____ costume.

4. Jack wore a white sheet with his

    (tsohg) _____ costume.

C. Wendy did her "Backward Spell" on the word for each loot bag too. Put the letters in order and find what is in each bag.

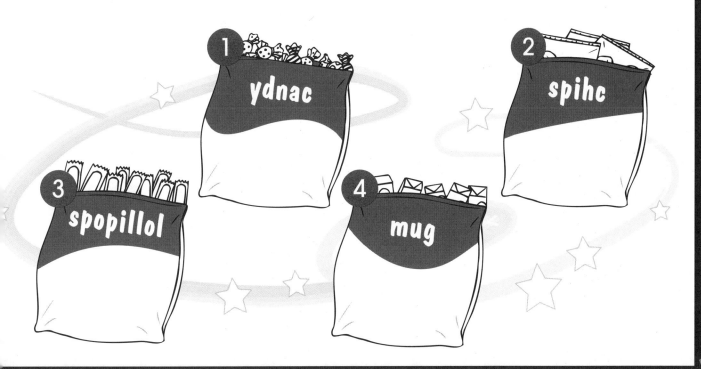

Long Vowels – Review

A. Use the same long vowel to complete all the words in each group.
Say the words.

1.
m___le
c___te
bl___e
p___pil

2.
t___me
d___ce
w___se
p___lot

3.
c___ve
bl___me
b___sin
t___pe

4.
r___w
j___ke
st___ne
p___st

B. Change the long vowels of the words to form new words. Write
them in the boxes. Draw lines to join the new words to the pictures.

1. pope

2. mole

3. cane

4. tales

5. like

6. coke

A
B
C
D
E
F

C. Say the things. Unscramble the words and write them next to the pictures. Circle ⃝ the long vowels in the words.

1.
   s i h s u

2.
   n w d w o i

3.
   s b b a a l l e

4.
   g t a i l a o l r

5.
   l p e a p n e i p

6.
   p o i p h

7.
   t i p u l

8.
   g w h h a y i

Day
45

Animal Homes

The forest is home for a moose or a deer.
A hive is home for a bee.
Rabbits and moles like to live in the ground.
A squirrel makes its home in a tree.

A pond is home for a fish or a frog.
A whale makes its home in the sea.
A fox or a bear will live in a den.
A farm can be home to a pig in a pen.

Each animal needs its own place to stay,
Where it can find food and keep danger away.

A. Circle ◯ the word that rhymes with the one on the left.

1. bear	wear	ear	pea
2. ground	round	pond	group
3. whale	wash	where	sail
4. hive	give	five	nine

B. Draw a line to help each animal find its home.

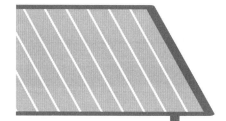

1. hive
2. hole
3. forest
4. tree
5. sea
6. pond
7. pen
8. den

Nouns (1)

Date : _____

A **noun** is a word that names an animal, a person, place, or thing.

Examples: horse (an animal)
teacher (a person)
park (a place)
doll (a thing)

A. Look at each picture and unscramble the word.

1. souhe

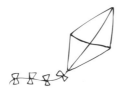

2. tike

1. _____

2. _____

3. _____

4. _____

5. _____

6. _____

3. dearb

4. titmen

7. _____

8. _____

9. _____

5. babirt

6. hocols

7. woc

8. sruen

9. ssalg

B. Put the nouns into the correct boxes.

Person
_____
_____
_____
_____

Animal
_____
_____
_____
_____

Place
_____
_____
_____
_____

Thing
_____
_____
_____
_____

house
kite
school
cow
beaver
bread
mother
mitten
driver
rabbit
jam
beach
nurse
man
moose
park

C. Circle ◯ the nouns in the sentences.

1. The boy is flying a kite.

2. The girl is eating an apple.

3. My dog is under the table.

4. The baby smiles.

5. The fish swims in the river.

6. The cat likes milk.

All Kinds of Homes

People live in many kinds of homes. Read about the homes and then find a picture of each home on the next page.

Highrise – a tall building with apartments on each floor

Two-storey house – a house with an upstairs and a downstairs level

Bungalow – a house with only one level

Town house – a house that is in a row of other houses

Trailer home – a house that can be moved to another place

Houseboat – a boat that people live on

A. Write the name for each kind of home.

1.

2.

3.

4.

5.

6.

B. Write the kind of home you live in and where it is.

_____

_____

Day
48

Nouns (2)

A. Look at these words. Some are nouns and some are not. Colour the nouns.

carrot	eat	chilly	star	boat
table	water	write	worker	grass
make	dim	singer	song	bag

B. Write the nouns you can see in the picture.

1. b___ ___l
2. b___ ___e
3. m___ ___
4. w___ ___ ___n
5. b___ ___d
6. t___ ___ ___
7. d___ ___
8. b___ ___ ___h
9. b___y
10. g___ ___l
11. k___ ___e
12. d___ ___l

C. Write three nouns on each card.

Place

Thing

Person

Animal

Use two
nouns from the
cards to make
a sentence.

Date : _____

Day

49

The Man in the Moon

Have you ever looked up at the moon at night?

When the moon looks like a complete circle, we say it is a full moon. The full moon has shadows that look like a face. People call this face "the man in the moon". There are many stories and poems about the man in the moon.

A. Fill in the missing words to complete this poem about the man in the moon.

high

moon

soon

sky

I saw the moon up in the _____ .

I looked at that moon, way up _____ !

I saw the face of a man in that big _____ .

I hope to see it again, very _____ !

B. Circle ◯ the correct words or fill in the blanks to finish these rhymes about the moon and the star.

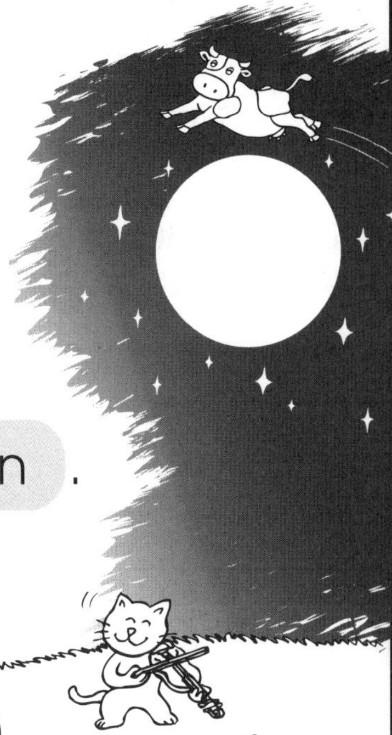

Hey diddle, diddle,

The cat and the 1. fiddle / little ,

The cow jumped over the 2. moon / spoon .

The little dog laughed to see such sport,

And the dish ran away with the 3. loon / spoon .

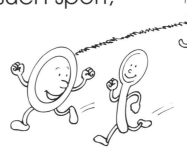

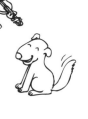

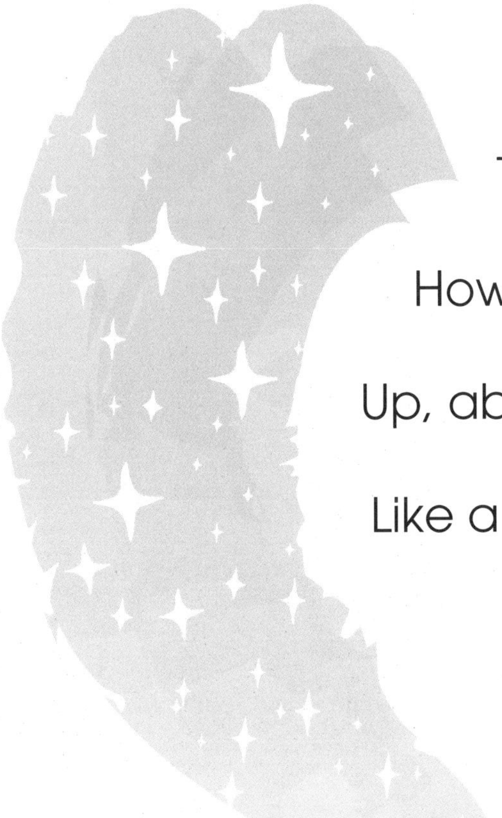

Twinkle, twinkle, little 4. ______________

How I wonder what you are.

Up, above the world, so high,

Like a diamond in the 5. ______________

Did You Know?

"Orange" and "silver" are the only words that do not rhyme with any other words in the English language.

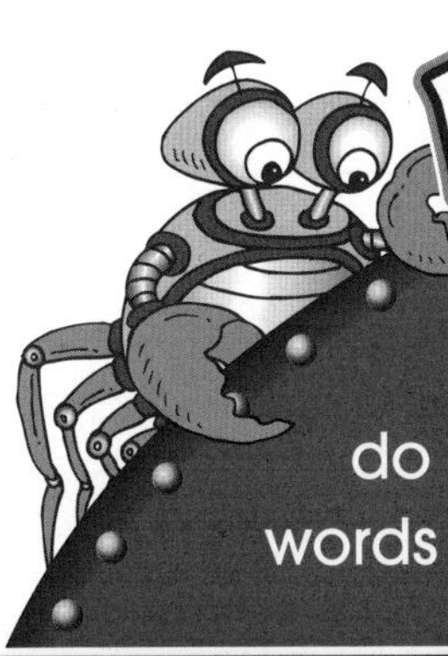

You Deserve A Break!

Jenny will not go out with the prince in Giantland unless he can find all the flowers and vegetables that have words with a long "e" sound. Help the prince by colouring what he has to find.

forest

petal

pea

farm

beet

field

lettuce

feast

pumpkin

dandelion

Nouns (3)

Common and Proper Nouns

A **common noun** names any person, animal, place, or thing.

Examples: doctor (person)   dog (animal)
            country (place)   apple (thing)

A **proper noun** names a specific person, animal, place, or thing. It always begins with a capital letter.

Examples: Dr. Jones (person)   Dalmatian (animal)
            Canada (place)   Red Delicious (thing)

A. Read the nouns. Put them in the correct cheese. Begin the proper nouns with capital letters.

car   rideau canal   butterfly   internet   halifax
school   kim   golden retriever   teacher   mouse

Common Nouns

_____
_____
_____
_____

Proper Nouns

_____
_____
_____
_____

Days of the week, months of the year, and festivals are proper nouns. They always begin with capital letters.

Examples: <u>Monday</u> is the second day of the week.

<u>Halloween</u> is in <u>October</u>.

B. Fill in the blanks with the correct proper nouns. Begin them with capital letters.

1. The 25th of _____ is _____ .

2. School starts in _____ .

3. The candy shop is closed on the weekend, that is _____ and _____ .

4. The first day of _____ is _____ .

5. Children eat chocolate eggs at _____ .

6. _____ is the third day of the week.

7. Tulips bloom in _____ .

8. _____ is the eighth month of the year.

sunday

tuesday

saturday

january

may

august

september

december

christmas

easter

new year's day

Date : _____

Planet Ex

I am about to blast off to my very own planet and I will name it Planet Ex.

My planet will have three big stores where everything is free. One store will be called "Foodarama" and it will be filled with all our favourite foods. Another store will be named "Clothes For Us" and it will give away all the cool things kids like to wear. The third store will have toys and computers for everyone, and its name will be "Toyco".

On Planet Ex there will be a playground and swimming pool on every street. Every week there will be a big party for everybody. Planet Ex will be a happy place where all people are friends.

A.   Choose a word from the planet that matches the words below.

planet
playground
party

1.   food, balloons, prizes

_____

2.   swing, slide, ladder

_____

3.   Mars, Jupiter, Earth

_____

B.   Sort the items and write the words for the correct store.

apple
socks
Tamagotchi
jeans
pizza
hat
cake
football
milk
crayon
shirt
computer

Nouns (4)

Singular and Plural Nouns

A **singular noun** names one person, animal, place, or thing.

Examples: girl, beaver, park, pencil

A **plural noun** names more than one person, animal, place, or thing. Many plural nouns are formed by adding "s" to the singular nouns.

Examples: girls, beavers, parks, pencils

A. Circle ◯ the word that best describes each picture.

1.

flower / flowers

2.

owl / owls

3.

castle / castles

4.

kid / kids

5.

clown / clowns

6.

pet / pets

B. Look at each picture. Draw a picture to make it plural in the box. Write the plural noun by adding "s" to the singular noun.

1.

mushroom

_____

2.

bear

_____

3.

balloon

_____

4.

robot

_____

5.

star

_____

The Tooth Fairy

Once upon a time there was a little  named

Tara. She had a very wiggly front 2. ☺ . One

day Tara was eating an 3. 🍎 . Suddenly, she

noticed that her 4. ☺ had come out. She

ran inside to show her 5. 👩‍👧 . Her mother gave

her a little 6. 📦 to put her 7. ☺ in.

That night, Tara put the 8. 📦 under her 9. 🛏 . She made a

wish that the tooth 10. 🧚 would come. In the morning,

she looked in the 11. 📦 . Inside, she found a shiny silver

coin. The tooth 12. 🧚 had given Tara

two dollars for

her 13. ☺ .

A. Use these words to replace the pictures in the story of The Tooth Fairy.

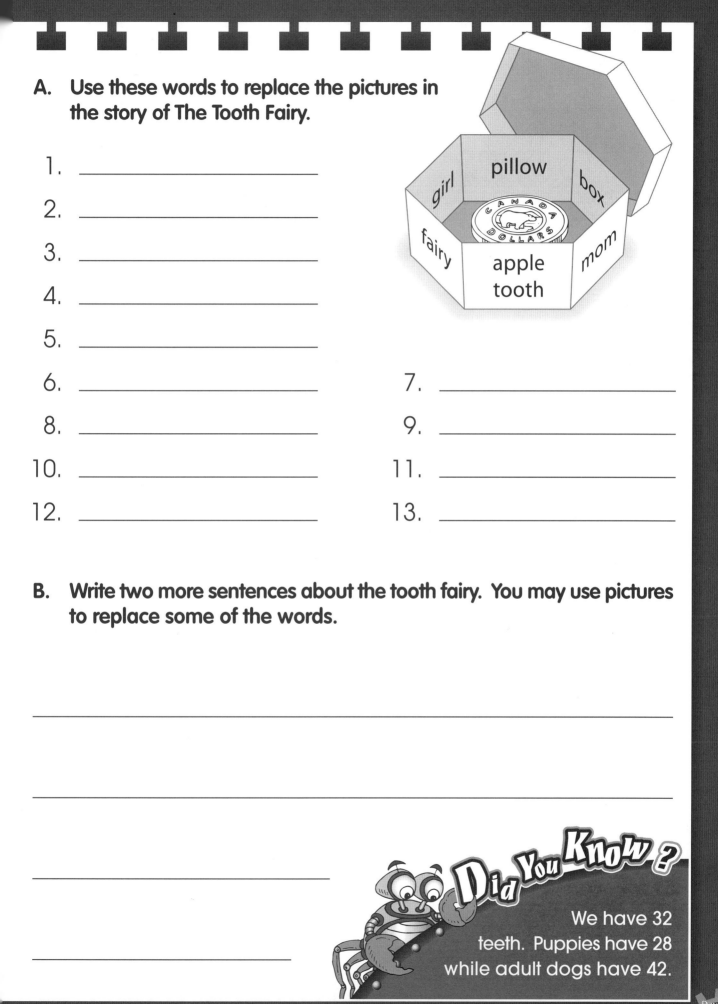

1. _____

2. _____

3. _____

4. _____

5. _____

6. _____   7. _____

8. _____   9. _____

10. _____   11. _____

12. _____   13. _____

girl   pillow   box   fairy   CANADA DOLLARS   apple   tooth   mom

B. Write two more sentences about the tooth fairy. You may use pictures to replace some of the words.

_____

_____

_____

_____

Did You Know?

We have 32 teeth. Puppies have 28 while adult dogs have 42.

Date : _____

Day 55

Nouns (5)

Plural Nouns

Some **plural nouns** are formed by adding "es" to the singular nouns.

If a noun ends in "s", "x", "ch", or "sh", add "es" to form its plural.

Examples: cross → crosses   peach → peaches

A. Change each singular noun to plural by adding "es". Write the plural noun under the correct picture.

| watch | box | sandwich | glass | dish | dress |

1.

2.

3.

4.

5.

6.

B. Fill in the blanks with the plural form of the given nouns.

1. The two (fox) _____ are playing in the forest.

2. There are so many (switch) _____ here. Which one should I press?

3. I put my friends' (address) _____ in this book.

4. There are two cats behind the (bush) _____ .

5. The (bus) _____ stop outside the school.

6. How many (bench) _____ are there in this park?

C. Look at each picture. Draw a picture to make it plural. Write the plural noun.

 brush

 witch

 octopus

_____   _____   _____

Dentist Dan

Alex and Anna have a special dentist. It is their Uncle Dan. Today they are going for a check-up. Uncle Dan checks their teeth and reminds them to brush twice a day. They each get a new toothbrush and toothpaste that is bubble gum flavour.

Anna gets a Barbie toothbrush and Alex gets one with SpongeBob. The children say thank you to their uncle. They can't wait to get home and try out their new toothpaste and toothbrushes!

A. Find words from the story to fill in the blanks.

1. A doctor who takes care of your teeth is a _____ .

2. Alex and Anna went for a _____ .

3. The flavour of the _____ was bubble gum.

4. The children each got a new _____ with a picture on it.

5. We should _____ our teeth twice a day.

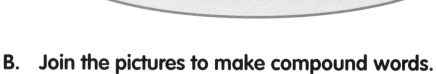

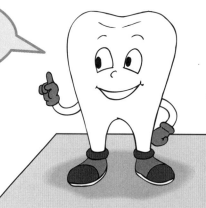

A compound word is made when two smaller words are joined to make a new word. "Toothbrush" and "toothpaste" are compound words.

B. Join the pictures to make compound words. Write the compound words in the boxes.

1.  +  →

2.  + →

3. 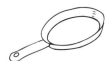 +  →

4. + →

5. +  →

6. +  →

7. + →

8. + →

Date : _____

Day
57

Sentences (1)

A **sentence** is a group of words. It tells a complete thought about someone or something. A sentence begins with a capital letter and ends with a period (.).
Example: We like playing basketball.

A. Read each group of words. Colour ☺ if it forms a sentence. Colour ☹ if it does not.

1. The little kitten.

2. Grandma is baking muffins.

3. Nina gives.

4. They work out in the gym.

5. Is delicious.

6. Jake wants to win the race.

7. Corn on the cob.

8. They laughed.

9. Penguins live in cold weather.

B. Read the sentences. Match them with the correct pictures by writing the letters in the boxes.

A. Carrie doesn't know the answer.

B. The boy has a funny mask.

C. The house looks scary.

D. Pandas like bamboo shoots.

E. The children are cheering loudly.

1. ☐

2. ☐

3. ☐

4. ☐

5. ☐

C. Rewrite the following as sentences.

1. i like chewing gum

_____

2. we buy gum in a candy shop

_____

3. bubble gum has many flavours

_____

_____

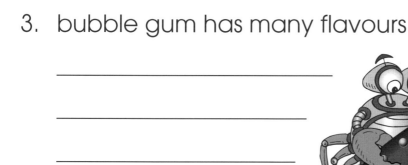

Did You Know?

The largest gum bubble was 23 inches in diameter. It was blown by a girl in 1994.

Looking at Maps

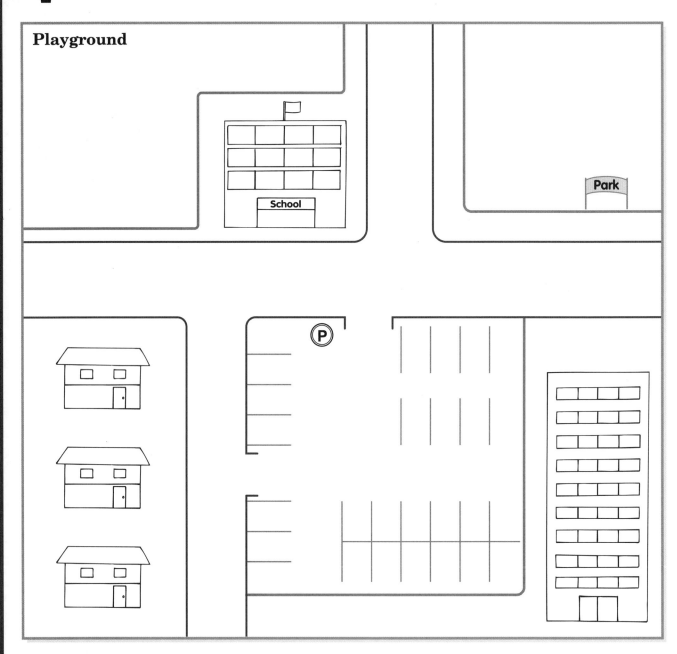

A. Read the instructions and draw the things on the map above.

- Draw a swing and a slide in the playground.
- Draw trees and flowers in the park.
- Draw some cars in the parking lot.
- Draw a bus outside the school.

B. Look at the maps and choose a title for each. Write the title on the line.

Canada
Riverside Park
Maple Street School
Newtown

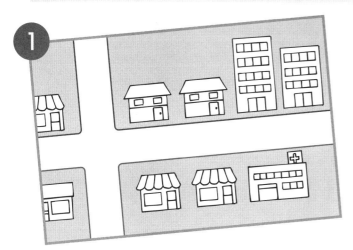

_____

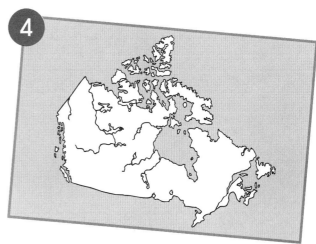

_____   _____

Sentences (2)

Subjects

The **subject** tells whom or what the sentence is about.

Example: Dolphins live in the sea.

In this sentence, "dolphins" is the subject.

A.   Underline the subject in each sentence.

1. Grandpa and Grandma are visiting us this winter.

2. The school bus stops in front of the house.

3. Monkeys like swinging from tree to tree.

4. Nina hid the lollipop under her pillow.

5. The duck is quacking loudly.

6. Rome is the capital of Italy.

7. The dog has five puppies.

8. Summer starts in June.

9. Zeta and Alice walk their dog together after school.

10. The aliens fly the spaceship.

B. Draw a line to match each subject with the rest of the sentence.

1.  The snake •

2.  The balloon •

3.  The CN Tower •

4.  The clock •

5. 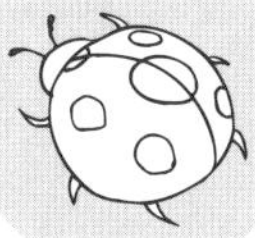 The ladybug •

• **A** is up in the sky.

• **B** is very tiny.

• **C** is ticking loudly.

• **D** is in Toronto.

• **E** is slithering in the grass.

C. Look at each picture and complete the sentence.

1 **2** **3**

1. The clown _____ .

2. The frog _____ .

3. Dad _____ .

You Deserve A Break!

The fairies have just turned the twins into flowers. They will grant the twins a second wish if they find the noun on each petal. Can you circle ◯ it for them?

high
forehead
twinkling

1

big
young
friend

2

tiny
hair
cute

3

4

chubby
cheeks
shiny

up
down
wings

5

fairy
dreamy
small

6

7

wand
wide
far

8

look
forgive
window

Bird Watching with Grandpa

My grandpa lives all by himself in an apartment building. There are tall trees outside his window and it's a great place for watching birds. When I visit Grandpa, he tells me the names of the birds. There are blue jays, cardinals, and robins. He lets me use his binoculars so I can see better.

Last year we saw a nest made of mud, grass, and twigs. There were three little eggs in the nest. The eggs were a greenish-blue colour. Grandpa told me that they were a robin's eggs. When the eggs hatched, we saw the mother robin bring bugs and worms to feed the babies. Bird watching with Grandpa is a very interesting hobby.

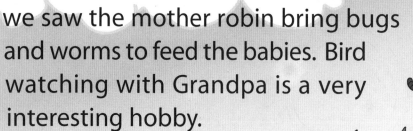

A. Name three kinds of birds in the story.

1. _____   2. _____

3. _____

B. Tell three things used to build a bird's nest.

1. _____   2. _____   3. _____

C. Arrange the words to make sense. Write the correct sentence on the line.

1. My   apartment   in   lives   grandpa   an

_____

2. We   watch   to   like   birds   the

_____

3. The   were   pretty   a   colour   eggs

_____

4. I   binoculars   to   used   better   see

_____

D. Use the letters in each nest to make a word from the story.

1.

_____

2.

_____

3.

_____

4.

_____

5.

_____

6.

_____

Sentences (3)

Telling Sentences

A **telling sentence** tells about someone or something. It begins with a capital letter and ends with a period (.).

Example: The snowman has a scarf.

A. Colour ☐T☐ **if it is a telling sentence.**

1. They slept in the tent at night. |T|

2. Stanley Park is in Vancouver. |T|

3. Can I go with you? |T|

4. What's that in your hand? |T|

5. Are you serious? |T|

6. How lovely! |T|

7. They went fishing. |T|

8. Why are you crying? |T|

9. It is rainy today. |T|

10. Cecil likes dinosaurs. |T|

B. Write the telling sentences correctly. Begin with a capital letter and end with a period.

1. they put on a very good play

   _____

   _____

2. they will go for a walk

   _____

3. bruce is writing his journal

   _____

4. it snows in winter

   _____

5. julia has a fluffy dog

   _____

C. Look at the picture. Write three telling sentences about it.

1. _____

   _____

2. _____

   _____

3. _____

   _____

Day 63

Canada Day

Bang! Crash! Boom! Red, green, blue – it's the fireworks display for Canada Day. Every year we celebrate Canada's birthday on July 1. All across the country people fly Canada's flag with its red maple leaf. Some towns have parades and festivals. Many families have picnics and barbecues.

At night the sky is alive with bright colours and big sounds. When the fireworks end we feel a little sad that the celebration is over for another year.

A. Choose the correct word to complete each sentence. Write the word on the line.

1. The date for Canada Day is (June 1, July 1).

   _____

2. The colour of the maple leaf on the Canadian flag is (red, green).

   _____

3. Canada is the name of our (town, country).

   _____

4. We celebrate Canada Day with (fireworks, movies).

   _____

B. Choose a word to complete each sentence.

flags   red   party

colours   sounds

1. On Canada Day our family had a big _____ .

2. The decorations for Canada Day were white and _____ .

3. Did you hear the loud _____ of the fireworks?

4. I love the bright _____ of the fireworks.

5. People were waving _____ at the parade.

C. Write your own sentence telling why you like Canada Day.

I like Canada Day because _____

_____

_____

_____ .

Did You Know?

On Canada's first birthday, there were only four provinces. They were Ontario, Quebec, New Brunswick, and Nova Scotia.

Day 64

Sentences (4)

Asking Sentences

An **asking sentence** asks about someone or something. It begins with a capital letter and ends with a question mark (?).

Example: How much is the teddy bear?

A. **Check ✔ the box if it is an asking sentence. Cross ✗ the box if it is not.**

1. How awesome! ☐

2. Do you like skiing? ☐

3. The rabbit has red eyes. ☐

4. Why are you so sad? ☐

5. I don't know what to do. ☐

6. Hurry, or you'll be late! ☐

7. What can we buy in that shop? ☐

8. Are you joining the charity walk? ☐

9. How can we get down? ☐

B. Write the asking sentences correctly. Begin with a capital letter and end with a question mark.

1. do you go to that school

   _____

2. can I have a candy

   _____

3. is this your cap

   _____

C. Fill in the blanks and add question marks to form asking sentences. Use each word only once.

| where | when | which | who |
| whose | why | how | are | does |

1. _____ cat do you like

2. _____ couldn't you come to the party

3. _____ did you go last Saturday

4. _____ your mother drive

5. _____ did you do that

6. _____ robot is this

7. _____ you sure you know the way

8. _____ is Thanksgiving Day

9. _____ likes vanilla ice cream

Family Picnic

My name is Rajinder Gill and my grandparents moved to Canada from India. Every year our family has a big picnic on Canada Day. When all the aunts, uncles, and cousins get together, we have over 20 people.

We go to a big park and enjoy soccer, kite flying, and badminton. When it is time to eat, the kids have hot dogs, chips, and pop. The grown-ups prefer chicken and salads, but we all enjoy the big Canada Day cake.

When it gets dark, we watch the fireworks display with all the other families at the park. Canada Day is a great day to celebrate with my family.

A.   Arrange the words to make sense. Write the correct sentence on the lines.

1. We   on   the   to   Canada   park   Day   went

   _____

   _____

2. We   together   Canada   Day   to   celebrate   get

   _____

   _____

B. **Choose the correct answer. Write the word on the line.**

1. Rajinder's grandparents came from _____ .

   Ireland   India   Italy

2. They play a game of _____ .

   school   slide   soccer

3. The children have _____ to drink.

   milk   pop   juice

4. The grown-ups eat salads and _____ .

   chicken   cheese   chocolate

5. When it gets dark, they watch _____ .

   television   fireworks   movies

Date : _____

Sentences (5)

Exclamatory Sentences

An **exclamatory sentence** shows strong emotion like fear, anger, or excitement. It begins with a capital letter and ends with an exclamation mark (!).

Example: Wow! It's gorgeous!

A. Check ✔ the exclamatory sentences.

1. Why shouldn't I touch it?   ◯

2. We finally won!   ◯

3. Can somebody help me?   ◯

4. Let's go.   ◯

5. The children are in the park.   ◯

6. How pretty!   ◯

7. Come here.   ◯

8. Is it true?   ◯

9. Help!   ◯

10. Ouch! It hurts!   ◯

B. Write the exclamatory sentences correctly. Begin with a capital letter and end with an exclamation mark.

1. how exciting

   _____

2. oh dear

   _____

3. what a surprise

   _____

4. watch your step

   _____

C. Look at each picture. Write an exclamatory sentence to go with it.

1. _____

2. _____

3. _____

4. _____

Best Buddies

Oliver and Katie are twins. They are just one year old. They came to visit their cousins in Toronto. Everyone noticed how happy they are.

They love to play with building blocks and Oliver laughs out loud when he knocks over the tower. Katie likes to climb into the toy box and throw the blocks out, one at a time. They both enjoy mealtime and eat lots of healthy food.

At bedtime they listen to their favourite book "Goodnight Moon". They are so lucky to have a best buddy to play with.

A. Answer the questions.

1. What are the names of the twins?

    _____ , _____

2. Where do their cousins live?   _____

3. What is their favourite book?   _____

4. Why are the twins lucky?

    _____

The word "twins" means that there are two babies born at the same time. The pictures below show some other things that come in "twos".

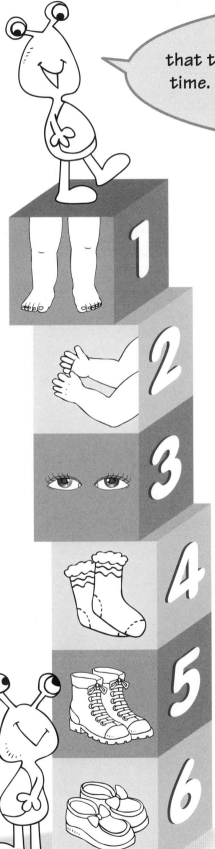

B. Write the correct word for each picture.

arms   legs   eyes

shoes   boots   socks

1. _____

2. _____

3. _____

4. _____

5. _____

6. _____

Punctuation and Capitalization

Punctuation

All sentences end with **punctuation marks**.

– A telling sentence ends with a period (.).
   Example: She is my friend.

– An asking sentence ends with a question mark (?).
   Example: Where's Celia?

– An exclamatory sentence ends with an exclamation mark (!).
   Example: It's incredible!

A. **Put the correct punctuation in the circles.**

1. You have my word on this 〇

2. Watch out 〇

3. Take a look over there 〇

4. See you 〇

5. I'll be back in an hour 〇

6. You did it 〇

7. Can you imagine that 〇

8. What's up 〇

9. What an awful thing 〇

10. It's just awesome 〇

11. How ridiculous 〇

Capitalization

All sentences begin with capital letters.
All proper nouns begin with capital letters.
Examples: The Wizard of Oz is an interesting
                    story.
                    Kyle likes this story very much.

B.   Follow the above rules and rewrite the sentences.

1. tyra named her dog casey.

   _____

   _____

2. the gardners went to italy for a holiday.

   _____

3. thanksgiving day is in october.

   _____

4. ian lives on scottfield cresent.

   _____

5. how did jason get the key?

   _____

6. roald dahl wrote "charlie and the chocolate factory".

   _____

   _____

Robby Raccoon Finds a Friend

One day Robby Raccoon went walking in the forest. He was looking for someone to play with. He met a little mouse sitting under a log.

Robby said, "Little mouse, will you play with me?"

"No," said the mouse. "Raccoons eat mice!" And the mouse ran away.

Next, Robby met a bird sitting in a tree. Robby said, "Bird, will you play with me?"

"No," said the bird. "Raccoons eat birds!" And the bird flew away.

So Robby Raccoon went down to the pond. He saw a frog sitting on a lily pad. He said, "Frog, will you play with me?"

"No," said the frog. "Raccoons eat frogs!" And the frog jumped away.

Finally, Robby decided to play by himself in the leaves. Suddenly, he noticed another raccoon playing there too. They began to run and jump in the leaves and chase each other. It was so much fun. Robby was very happy he had finally found a friend!

A. **Put the events in order by writing the letters on Robby Raccoon's tail.**

(A) Robby met a bird.

(B) Robby met another raccoon.

(C) Robby met a frog.

(D) Robby met a mouse.

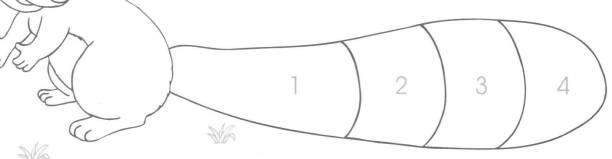

1   2   3   4

B. **Unscramble the words and write them in the blanks.**

1. The (brdi) _____ was sitting in a tree.

    Then it (felw) _____ away.

2. The (forg) _____ was sitting on a lily pad.

    Then it decided to (pumj) _____ away.

3. The (seoum) _____ was sitting under a log.

    Then it (nar) _____ away.

4. Robby (Rooacnc) _____ was walking in the forest.

    Then he (dounf) _____ a friend.

Date : _____

Day 70

You Deserve A Break!

What animals do you see? Find and circle ◯ their names in the word search.

k	a	p	n	v	b	j	c	g	d
b	m	e	l	g	r	x	u	o	a
h	i	l	o	w	t	f		s	i
j	c	u	b	k	m	i	n	v	e
r	s	o	s	l	j	i	x	j	g
q	m		t	b	o	a	p	e	r
s	t	y	e	g	w	l	u	l	h
t	d	v	r	z	w	h	a	l	e
a	k	p	y	t	c	h	v	y	m
r	f	i	s	h	z	i	d	f	o
f	e	q	l	u	t	s		i	k
i	n	a	g	p	e	j	w	s	s
s	i	z	j	x	y	q	t	h	b
h	l	f	t		e	h	a	m	i
r	n	i	x	v	u	t	o	c	g
b	h	k	v	s	h	a	r	k
s	h	e	l	d	w	k	i	l

h	m	l	d	k	b	e	o	a	g
e	a	j	q	h	s	f	o	j	n
k	g	n	c	o	p		c	r	f
b	c	p	l	s	e	r	t	k	a
m	f	b	a	t	u	m	o	d	i
t	l	w	m	y	c	v	p	t	g
u	j	r	o	e	s	q	u	i	d
r	c	g	a	i	v	z	s	p	h
t	o	t	u	q	b	s	x	n	c
l	u	f		z	j	h	o	t	l
e	s	e	a	h	o	r	s	e	p
n	q	d	k	c	s	i	d	r	m
e	a	o	g	w	v	m	j		h
r	m		u	o	l	p	f	e	a
i	b	t	j	c	r	a	b	m	i
h	s	d	s	g	k	r	r		c
l	c	o	i		e	s			v

Word Order in Sentences

Sentences need to make sense. The order of the words in a sentence can change the meaning of the sentence.

Example: The dog ate the bone.
             The bone ate the dog.

A.   Read each pair of sentences. Check ✔ the one that makes sense.

1. The car stole the robbers.

    The robbers stole the car.

2. Jamie put the cat in the basket.

    Jamie put the basket in the cat.

3. The table is sitting at the children.

    The children are sitting at the table.

4. Sharon turned on the computer.

    The computer turned on Sharon.

5. My sister goes to Westside School.

    Westside School goes to my sister.

6. The curtains are drawing Lester.

    Lester is drawing the curtains.

B. Look at the picture. Rewrite the sentences so that they make sense.

1. The sky is in the bird.

   _____

2. The chicks are feeding the boys.

   _____

3. Big baskets have the boys.

   _____

C. Put the words in order to make sentences.

1. ate   big   ice cream   a   Josh   bowl   of

   _____

   _____

2. are   at   They   rink   skating   the

   _____

   _____

Date : _____

Day
72

My Dad Is the Best

My dad is the best,
From the east to the west.

He hugs me tight,
When I'm scared at night.

We go out and play,
On a sunny day.

Sometimes we play ball,
Or shop at the mall.

Together we cook,
Or read a good book.

When he takes me to school,
I think it's so cool.

I'm very glad,
That I have a great dad!

A. Write the rhyming words that end each verse of the poem. Then, think of one more rhyming word for each line.

A good way to think of rhyming words is to go through the alphabet in your mind until you come to a word that fits the rhyme you need.

Rhyming Words in the Poem

1. _____ _____
2. _____ _____
3. _____ _____
4. _____ _____
5. _____ _____
6. _____ _____
7. _____ _____

Your Own Rhyming Words

_____
_____
_____
_____
_____
_____
_____

B. Write two lines of one more thing you and your dad do together. Make the lines rhyme.

_____

_____

Pronouns

He, She, It, and They

A **pronoun** is a word that replaces a noun. "He", "she", "it", and "they" are some of the pronouns.

Examples: Colin has a new robot.

It is blue and red in colour.

He likes it very much.

In the second sentence, "it" replaces the "new robot". In the third sentence, "he" replaces "Colin".

A. Write the correct pronoun under each picture.

1    2    3    4

_____   _____   _____   _____

B. Fill in the blanks with the correct pronouns.

1. The boys had a game of soccer. _____ are very tired now.

2. Audrey has a dog. _____ walks it in the park every day.

3. There is an apple on the table. _____ is big.

4. Ken is sad. _____ has lost his favourite toy car.

I, You, and We

"I" is used when you are talking about yourself.

"You" is used when you are talking to another person.

"We" is used when you are talking about yourself and another person or other people.

Examples: I'm going hiking this Sunday.

Will <u>you</u> join me?

<u>We</u> can set out in the morning.

C. Write pronouns to replace the pictures on the lines.

Kathy and 1. went

hiking last week. 2. walked by a creek. 3.

saw some ducks in there. 4. wanted to take a better

look of them, but 5. tripped over a stone and fell into

the water. Kathy laughed. To hide my embarrassment,

6. said, "It's so very hot today. 7. just wanted to

take a cool bath in the water. Would 8. like to join

me?"

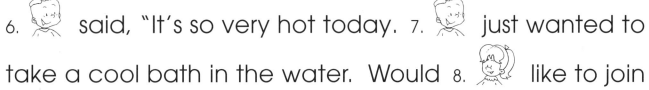

1. _____   2. _____   3. _____   4. _____

5. _____   6. _____   7. _____   8. _____

Hairy Harry

Make a funny present for Dad. It can be for Father's Day, his birthday, or just any day of the year!

What you need:

- a styrofoam cup
- a cup of soil
- seeds (grass or alfalfa)
- a pair of scissors
- markers or glue and coloured paper

What you do:

1. Decorate the cup with eyes, nose, and mouth using markers or shapes cut out from paper.

2. Fill the cup with soil.

3. Plant seeds in the soil.

4. Place the cup in a sunny place and water the soil.

Fill in the missing vowels to complete the words.

I made a funny 1. pr__s__nt for my

dad. I got a styrofoam 2. c__p and

put a face on it. I drew a 3. r__d mouth,

glued on a 4. bl__ck nose and two 5. bl__e eyes. Then I

6. pl__nted some 7. gr__ss seeds in the 8. c__p . I made

sure the plant had 9. s__n and 10. w__ter . Soon the

seeds began to 11. gr__w . It looked 12. l__ke a funny

man 13. w__th long hair. My dad began 14. t__ laugh

when he saw it. He gave me a big 15. h__g and said

16. "th__nk you" for the

17. f__nny 18. pr__s__nt .

Did You Know?

All plants
need light, water,
air, and nutrients to grow.

Verbs (1)

A **verb** is an action word. It tells what someone or something does.

Example: A clown <u>does</u> funny tricks.

A. **Draw lines to join the verbs to the pictures.**

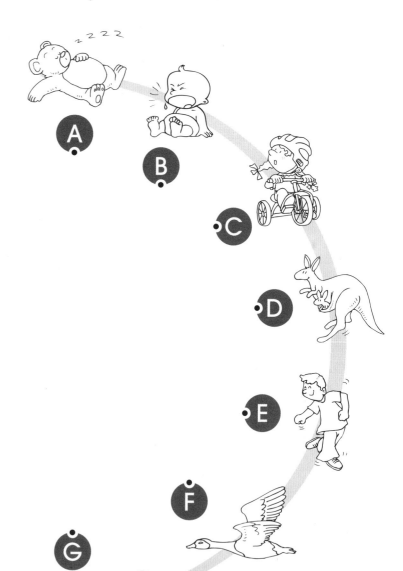

1. cries •

2. hops •

3. dances •

4. chases •

5. flies •

6. sleeps •

7. cycles •

B. Underline the verbs in the sentences.

1. This bus goes to the train station.

2. Bees collect nectar from flowers.

3. The chef works in that hotel.

4. Rosanne likes eating tortilla chips.

5. Mom reads me a story every night.

6. We give presents to one another at Christmas.

C. Look at the picture. Complete the verbs. Circle ◯ the actions in the picture.

1. p___ ___y

2. s___i___

3. sh___ ___ ___s

4. b___ ___ ___d

5. p___c___

6. c h___ ___

7. r___ ___

8. s___ ___b___t___e

Animal Tails

Have you ever noticed that animals have tails of many shapes and sizes? Some animals have special uses for their tails.

A fox can use its bushy tail to curl up and keep warm.

A squirrel's tail can act as a parachute to help it jump through the treetops.

A cow uses its tail to chase away pesky insects.

A beaver uses its flat tail to slap the water as a loud signal.

A lizard sheds its tail to avoid an enemy and can then grow a new one.

Fish, of course, use their tails to swim.

A.   Circle ◯ the word that rhymes with the one on the left.

1. tail   tell   sail   wall

2. cow   low   tow   now

3. slap   sleep   clap   sled

4. curl   cure   pearl   purr

B. Choose the matching tail for each animal.

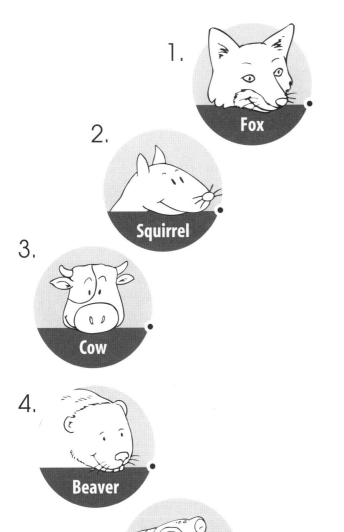

1. Fox
2. Squirrel
3. Cow
4. Beaver
5. Lizard
6. Fish

A uses its tail to signal

B uses its tail to keep warm

C uses its tail to swim

D uses its tail to swat flies

E can grow a new tail

F uses its tail as a parachute

C. Think of an animal that does not have a tail.

_____

Date : _____

Day 77

Verbs (2)

Am, Is, and Are

"**Am**" is used with "I".

"**Is**" is used to tell about one person, animal, place, or thing.

"**Are**" is used to tell about more than one person, animal, place, or thing.

Example: The children <u>are</u> playing.

A. **Look at the pictures and read the sentences. Circle ◯ the correct words.**

1. The birds   am / is / are   singing.

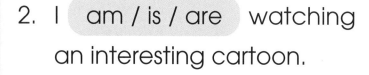

2. I   am / is / are   watching an interesting cartoon.

3. The dog   am / is / are   barking.

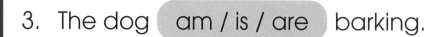

4. There   am / is / are   a happy face on the vest.

5. I   am / is / are   playing with my cat.

B. **Look at the picture. Fill in the blanks with "am", "is", or "are".**

1. There _____ a bike on the roof of the car.

2. I _____ walking behind my dad.

3. There _____ a hive in the tree.

4. The bees _____ flying around the hive.

5. It _____ a sunny day.

6. There _____ some apples in the tree.

7. I _____ waving at my friend.

8. Her dad _____ driving.

Date : _____

Beaver Tails

Have you ever eaten Beaver Tails? They are made of hot pastry with sugar on top. They are called Beaver Tails because they are flat and shaped like the tails of beavers.

Ottawa, the capital city of Canada, is famous for Beaver Tails. In winter people skate along the Rideau Canal in Ottawa. They like to eat Beaver Tails to warm them up after skating. Beaver Tails are good at any time but they are best on a cold winter day!

A. Write "Yes" if the sentence is true. Write "No" if the sentence is not true.

1. Ottawa is the capital of Canada. _____

2. Ottawa has warm weather all year. _____

3. Beaver Tails are a kind of food. _____

4. Beaver Tails are shaped like a ball. _____

5. People eat Beaver Tails after skating. _____

B. Circle ⃝ the correct word to complete each sentence.

1. Beaver Tails taste   sweet / sour   .

2. Beaver Tails are a kind of   pasta / pastry   .

3. The river freezes in   summer / winter   .

4. People eat   cold / hot   pastry to warm up.

5. People like to   swim / skate   on the Rideau Canal in Ottawa.

Did You Know?

The beaver uses its tail as a rudder or a diving plane while swimming in the water.

Date : _____

Verbs (3)

Past Tense Verbs

Some verbs tell about something that happened in the past.
Most verbs add "d" or "ed" to form the past tense.
Examples: bake → baked   climb → climbed

A. Circle ◯ the past tense verbs in the sentences.

1. The children jumped into the pool at once.

2. Mrs. Kenford walks her dog every day.

3. It rained heavily yesterday.

4. Oscar likes drawing on the walls.

5. I tied a big bow around the gift box.

6. We send a Christmas card to Grandpa and Grandma every year.

Some of them contain no past tense verbs.

7. Cheryl looked into the box and found the toonie.

8. They can have their lunch in the food court.

9. The girls shared the bag of potato chips.

10. Let's spend our holiday in Algonquin Park.

11. Ryan rolled the ball to his little sister.

B. Read the present tense verbs in Column A. Write them in the past tense in Column B.

1. dance

2. pick

3. watch

4. save

5. learn

_____

_____

_____

_____

_____

C. Look at the pictures. Fill in the blanks with the past tense verbs in (B).

1.

They _____ some flowers in the garden.

2.

Rex _____ money for a new video game.

3.

The girl _____ beautifully.

4.

The baby elephant _____ how to stand.

You Deserve A Break!

Help Willy and Amanda find nouns from the lily pads. Colour the lily pads with nouns. Write the nouns in the tree.

flower

lilies

long

white

grass

water

Marvin the Magician

A magician is a person who does clever tricks to entertain people. He often wears a tall hat and a big black cape. He can use the hat and cape to hide things for his magic tricks.

A magician usually has a magic wand. He waves it in the air as he says the magic words.

A. Finish the picture of "Marvin the Magician".

1. Add a top hat.

2. Give him a big cape.

3. Draw a magic wand in his left hand.

4. Write the word "Abracadabra" in the speech balloon.

Try this magic trick with your family and friends!

"Turn four pennies into five!"

- Put four pennies on the table.
- Push them off the table into one hand and close your hand.
- Say "Abracadabra" and open your hand.
- Then count the pennies. There are now five!

The secret:

Before you begin, use some tape to stick a penny under the table. As you push the four pennies into your hand, reach under the table and pull off the other penny.

B. Put the events in order by writing 1, 2, 3, and 4 on the lines.

_____ Put four pennies on the table.

_____ Stick one penny under the table before you start the trick.

_____ Say "Abracadabra" and show five pennies.

_____ Scoop the pennies into your hand.

Day
82

Adjectives (1)

An **adjective** tells about a noun (animal, person, place, or thing).
It often tells how an animal, a person, place, or thing looks.
Examples: a <u>cute</u> cat (an animal)
a <u>tall</u> girl (a person)
a <u>big</u> park (a place)
a <u>sharp</u> pencil (a thing)

A. Draw lines to join the adjectives to the nouns.

girl

weather

butterfly

plane

1. sad

2. cold

3. beautiful

4. stormy

5. fast

6. fat

drink

pig

B. Look at each picture. Find an adjective from the list that tells about the noun. Write it on the line.

| slow | fierce | soft | bright | long | crispy |

1 a _____ snake

2 a _____ pillow

3 a _____ dog

4 _____ crackers

5 a _____ snail

6 a _____ sun

C. Look at each picture. Write an adjective to tell about it.

1.
a _____
kitten

2.
a _____
chick

3.
a _____
Christmas tree

If I Had a Magic Wand...

Mrs. Green asked her grade one students to complete the following sentence.

"If I had a magic wand…"

These are what some children wrote.

Thomas: "If I had a magic wand, I'd make apple trees grow candy apples and all the flowers would be jelly beans."

Vicki: "If I had a magic wand, I'd make me and my brother fly so we could fly across the ocean and visit our grandparents."

Lucas: "If I had a magic wand, I'd make a toy store where all the toys would be free."

Nicole: "If I had a magic wand, I'd make lots of snow so we could make a snowman, slide down the hill, and build a snow fort."

A.   Finish the sentence with your own idea.

If I had a magic wand, _____

_____

_____ .

B. Circle ◯ the word in each sentence that has letters mixed up. Write the correct spelling on the line.

1. Thomas likes to aet jelly beans.   _____

2. Vicki would like to fyl across the ocean.   _____

3. Lucas would like to get some fere toys.   _____

4. Nicole loves to play in the snwo.   _____

C. Complete the rhymes with the words you wrote in (B).

1. The bird in the tree,

   Will fly away and be _____ .

2. When the north wind does blow,

   Then we shall have _____ .

3. Sometimes for a treat,

   We have candy to _____ .

4. Look up in the sky,

   To see the plane _____ .

Adjectives (2)

Some adjectives tell about the colour or number of people, animals, places, or things.

Examples: <u>three</u> strawberries
the <u>blue</u> sky

A. Colour or draw the pictures.

1. a yellow mango 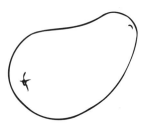	2. two lollipops
3. a blue kite 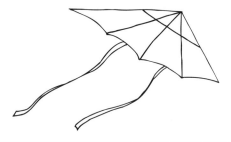	4. four stars
5. a brown teddy bear 	6. five apples

Some adjectives tell about the size or shape of nouns.

Examples: a <u>big</u> whale

an <u>oval</u> balloon

B.   Look at each picture. Find an adjective from the list that tells about the noun. Write what it is on the line.

1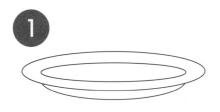

2

Adjectives

huge

tiny

round

square

oval

3

4

5

Nouns

bee

globe

dish

bear

mirror

1.   an _____

2.   _____

3.   _____

4.   _____

5.   _____

Niagara Falls

The Lee family went to Niagara Falls. They stayed at a hotel and their room had an awesome view of the Falls. In the morning they walked down to the Falls and had their pictures taken. Later they went on a boat called "The Maid of the Mist". It took them very close to the Falls and they got splashed.

After the boat ride, they walked up the hill to see all the shops and restaurants. Kim had cotton candy and Stephen had a waffle cone. Mrs. Lee bought some fudge to take home. Mr. Lee bought some postcards to send to his friends. Everyone got T-shirts with pictures of Niagara Falls. At night they saw an amazing fireworks display.

A. Arrange the words to make sense. Write the correct sentence on the line.

1. My   went   Falls   Niagara   family   to

   _____

2. exciting   The   was   ride   boat

   _____

3. The   was   fireworks   amazing   display

   _____

B. Put the events in order by writing 1, 2, 3, and 4 on the fireworks.

They bought treats.

They had their pictures taken.

They saw fireworks.

They went on a boat ride.

C. Write "Yes" if the sentence is true. Write "No" if the sentence is not true.

1. They had pictures taken by the Falls.   _____

2. "The Maid of the Mist" is a restaurant.   _____

3. They all got new T-shirts.   _____

4. Stephen got cotton candy.   _____

Prepositions

> A **preposition** tells about where an animal, a person, place, or thing is located.
>
> *Examples*: The cat is <u>behind</u> the TV.
> The mouse is <u>beside</u> the TV.

A. Write the correct preposition for each picture.

in	on	beside	behind	above	under

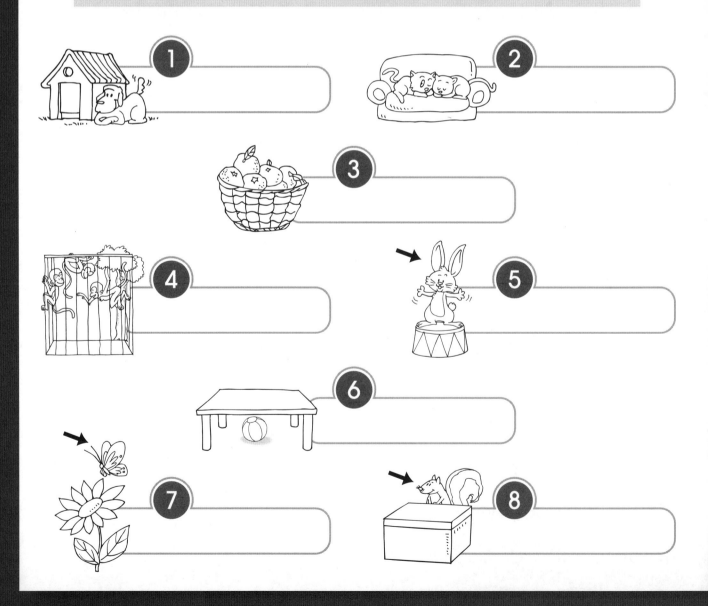

1. _____

2. _____

3. _____

4. _____

5. _____

6. _____

7. _____

8. _____

B. Read the directions and complete the picture.

- Draw a bird flying above the tree.
- Draw a girl sitting under the tree.
- Draw a boy playing on the swing.
- Draw a box on the grass.
- Draw a cat in the box.
- Draw a fountain behind the bushes.
- Draw some flowers beside the rock.
- Colour the picture.

My Summer Vacation

In September Mr. Patel asked his class to write about their summer vacations. Stephen Lee wrote about his trip to Niagara Falls.

In July my family went to Niagara Falls. On the first day we went on "The Maid of the Mist" and got splashed with water. At night we went to the Midway and did the Ghostblasters ride. We also saw a big fireworks display.

The next day we played mini golf at Dinosaur Park. We had lunch at the top of the Skylon Tower. We could see the Falls in all directions.

On the last day it was raining so we did indoor activities. We went to the Haunted House and the Wax Museum. There were so many attractions; we didn't have time to see them all. I hope we can go back to Niagara Falls again next year.

A. Arrange the words to make sense. Write the correct sentence on the line.

1. Stephen   about   vacation   summer   wrote   his

   _____

2. He   visit   again   to   wanted   Niagara Falls

   _____

B. Match the words that go together. Write the letter from the first list beside the correct match in the second list.

(A) colour and sound

(B) famous people

(C) restaurant

(D) exciting rides

(E) famous waterfalls

(F) scary ghosts

(G) boat ride

(H) mini golf

1. Dinosaur Park _____

2. Maid of the Mist _____

3. Fireworks Display _____

4. Haunted House _____

5. Wax Museum _____

6. Midway _____

7. Skylon Tower _____

8. Niagara Falls _____

Day
88

Articles

"A", "an", and "the" are **articles**. They come before nouns.
"A" is used before a noun that begins with a consonant.
"An" is used before a noun that begins with a vowel.
"The" is used before a noun that names a particular person, place, or thing.

Examples: <u>a</u> car   <u>an</u> apple   <u>the</u> Prime Minister

A.   Write the correct article for each noun.

1. _____ sky

2. _____ ostrich

3. _____ popsicle

4. _____ lion

5. _____ umbrella

6. _____ capital of Canada

7. _____ bracelet

8. _____ Atlantic Ocean

9. _____ owl

10. _____ Great Lakes

11. _____ ice cube

12. _____ party hat

B. **Look at each picture. Write what it is with the correct article.**

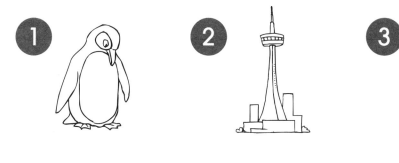

1. _____

2. _____

3. _____

4. _____

5. _____

6. _____

C. **Fill in the blanks with the correct articles.**

1. _____ nine planets revolve around _____ sun.

2. _____ earth is bigger than _____ moon.

3. _____ stars seem to form _____ oval shape.

4. We may see _____ shooting star.

5. _____ moon is the brightest object in _____ night sky.

Did You Know?

Some scientists believe they have found the tenth planet in our solar system.

Synonyms and Antonyms

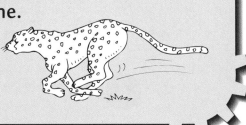

Synonyms

Synonyms are words that mean the same.

Examples: big – large
fast – quick
price – cost

A. Circle ◯ the word that is the synonym for each word on the left.

1. happy   sad   smile   glad   cheer

2. tall   thin   high   above   short

3. windy   blow   rainy   breezy   gust

4. jump   hop   dance   sit   stand

5. dark   black   dim   bright   light

B. Colour ☺ if they are synonyms. Colour ☹ if they are not.

1. stop – halt

2. year – calendar

3. smooth – rugged

4. thin – slim

5. pretty – beautiful

Antonyms

Antonyms are words that mean the opposite.

Examples: big – small
fast – slow
love – hate

C. Draw lines to join the words in the boxes to the pictures and match the antonyms.

1.    •

2.   •

3.   •

cold
tall
old
cheap
dirty
full

- expensive
- short
- hungry
- young
- clean
- hot

4.   •

5.    •

6.   •

You Deserve A Break!

Wow! Look at the words on Audrey's and Sydney's hair. Read what they say and write the correct words in the spaces provided.

purple

black

long

curly

straight

blue

brown

blonde

red

thick

Sydney, can you find all the colour words on my hair?

Sydney's Answers

_____   _____

_____   _____

_____

wobbly

wavy

giddy

messy

frizzy

pretty

thin

puffy

big

short

Sure I can! Can you find all the words with double consonants on my hair?

Audrey's Answers

_____   _____

_____   _____

1 Birthday Surprise

A. 1. C   2. A   3. E
    4. B   5. D
B. 1. six   2. kitten
    3. white   4. Snowball
C. 1. Midnight   2. Tiger
    3. Dusty   4. Socks

2 Beginning Consonants (1)

B. (Circle these pictures.)

D.

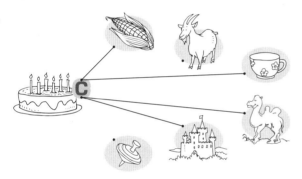

E. (Individual drawings)

3 A Thank You Letter

A. 1. book   2. animals
    3. monkeys   4. project
B. 1. The monkey is eating.
    2. The monkeys are in a cage.
    3. The book is about animals.

4 Beginning Consonants (2)

B. 1. d   2.   3. d
    4.   5. d   6. d
D. (Cross out these pictures.)
    1.   2.

    3.   4.

E. 1. f   2. d   3. d

5 Toast with Honey

A. 1. toaster   2. toasted
    3. toasting
B. 1. honey   2. jam
    3. cheese   4. butter
    5. ham
C. 1. honey   2. jam
    3. lunch   4. toast

6 Beginning Consonants (3)

B. (Circle these pictures.)

D. (Colour the ♡ of 1, 2, and 4.)
E. 1. h   2. g
    3. g   4. h

7 How Honey Is Made

A. 1. honeybee   2. beehive
B. 1. insect   2. flowers
    3. six   4. sweet
C. 1. bee   2. honeycomb
    3. honey   4. beehive

8 Beginning Consonants (4)

B.

D. (Colour these pictures.)

E. 1. jacket   2. kettle
    3. kitchen   4. jeep
    5. jellyfish   6. kayak

9 Number Rhymes

A. 1. two   2. four   3. six
    4. eight   5. ten
B. 1. Seven   2. Three
    3. five   4. five
    5. two   6. three
    7. four   8. four
    9. seven   10. twelve
   11. two   12. three

10 You Deserve A Break!

(Colour each pair of picture and word a different colour.)

 bagels   bananas   bus

 boots   bunny   bow

 beans   balloons   basket

11 Beginning Consonants (5)

B. (Cross out these pictures.)

D.

E.

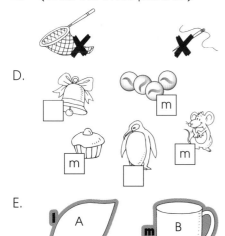

12 The Three Little Pigs

A. 1. No   2. No   3. Yes   4. Yes
B. 1. The wolf blew down the house of wood.
    2. The wolf climbed down the chimney.
    3. The wolf blew down the house of straw.
    4. The wolf fell into a pot of hot water.

13 Beginning Consonants (6)

B. (Colour these pictures.)

D. 1. parrot ; ✔   2. cape
    3. clip   4. piano ; ✔
E.

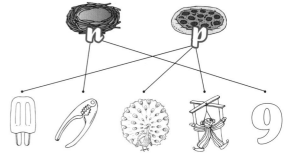

14 Kim's Rainbow

A. (Individual colouring of the rainbow)
B. (Individual colouring of the pictures)
    1. red   2. orange   3. yellow
    4. green   5. blue   6. purple

15 Beginning Consonants (7)

B. (Circle these pictures.)
    1.   2.   3.

D.

    rake ; rainbow ; raccoon ; rocks
E. 1. queen   2. rocket
    3. quack   4. rhino

16 Mixing Colours

A. (Individual colouring of the shapes)

1. 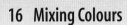 orange   2. green   3. purple

B. (Individual drawing)
1. black   2. black
3. black   4. black

17 Beginning Consonants (8)

B. (Draw these pictures in the sock.)

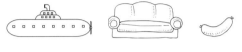

D. 1.   2. ✔   3. ✔   4. ✔
E.

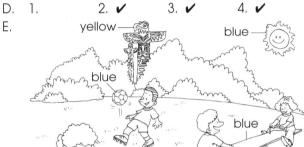

yellow   blue   blue   blue   blue   yellow   yellow

18 Breakfast Menu

Milk Products:
Yogurt ; Milk ; Cream cheese
Fruit and Vegetables:
Apple juice ; Banana ; Cranberry juice ; Orange juice
Meat Products:
Ham ; Sausage ; Bacon
Grain Products:
Waffles ; Pancakes ; Bagel ; Toast

19 Beginning Consonants (9)

B.

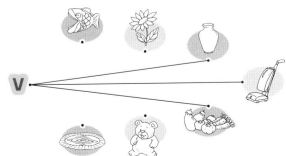

D. 1. whistle   2.
   3. watermelon   4.
   5. windmill   6. wallet
E. 1. w   2. v   3. v   4. w

20 You Deserve A Break!

1. airplane   2. bird
3. cow   4. earth
5. frog   6. goose
7. hippo   8. jam
9. kite   10. lemon
11. monkey   12. robin
13. tea   14. van
15. water   16. zebra

(Colour the ◯ with these words.)
bird ; cow ; frog ; goose ; hippo ; monkey ; robin ; zebra

21 Lunch at School

A. 1. Yes   2. No
   3. Yes   4. No
B. 1. fish   2. school
   3. hello   4. today
C. 1. lunch ; school   2. cheese
   3. sandwich   4. peach
   5. Each

22 Beginning Consonants (10)

B.

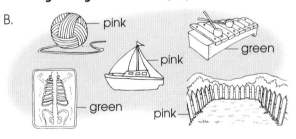

pink   green   pink   green   pink

D. z ero   z oo   z ig-zag   z ucchini

E. 1. zoom   2. yogurt
   3. yolk   4. zipper

3

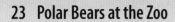

23 Polar Bears at the Zoo

A. 1. zoo   2. pool
    3. fish   4. window

B. 1.   2.

    3.   4.

C. 1. swim   2. fly
    3. run   4. hop

D. (Individual writing and drawing)

24 Ending Consonants (1)

A. (Colour the pictures of 1, 2, 3, 5, and 7.)

B. 1. c   2. b   3. d
    4. d   5. d   6. b
    7. f   8. b   9. f

25 Arctic Polar Bears

A. All About Polar Bears

B. 1. Yes   2. Yes   3. Yes
    4. No   5. Yes   6. Yes

C. 1. paws   2. cold
    3. white   4. food

26 Ending Consonants (2)

A. 1. m   2. l   3. g   4. m
    5. k   6. g

B. 1. k   2. g   3. m   4. k
    5. l   6. m   7. g   8. l
    9. k   10. k   11. l   12. g
    13. g   14. l   15. m   16. g
    17. l

27 Budgie Birds

A. 1. Budgie birds are good pets.
    2. They like to eat bird seed.
    3. The bird is in a cage.
    4. Budgie birds can learn to talk.

B. 1.   2.

3.   4.

C. 1. bark   2. swim
    3. fly   4. run

28 Ending Consonants (3)

A. 1. pear   2. glass   3. pin
    4. top   5. cactus   6. acorn
    7. soap   8. star

B. 1. octopu ; s   2. chai ; r
    3. crow ; n   4. tige ; r
    5. iro ; n   6. shee ; p
    7. spide ; r   8. snowma ; n
    9. rhinocero ; s   10. stam ; p

29 Grandma's Pet

A. (Individual colouring of the puffs of cream)

green   yellow   black

B. 1. bird   2. day
    3. grandma   4. cage
    5. pet

C. 1. Yes   2. Yes   3. No
    4. No   5. Yes

30 You Deserve A Break!

happy ; face ; ribbon ; marbles ; beads ; corn ; chips ; lemon ; peels

1. ribbon ; happy ; face
2. marbles ; ribbon ; happy ; face
3. corn ; chips ; pretty ; marbles ; ribbon ; happy ; face
4. lemon ; peels ; corn ; chips ; pretty ; marbles ; ribbon ; happy ; face
5. strings ; of ; beads ; lemon ; peels ; corn ; chips ; pretty ; marbles ; ribbon ; happy ; face

31 Ending Consonants (4)

A. 1. w   2. y   3. t   4. x
    5. t   6. x   7. w   8. y

B. 1. h o c k e (y)   2. m a i l b o (x)
    3. t e a p o (t)   4. r a i n b o (w)

5. hea r(t)   6. sa(w)
7. rocke(t)   8. tra(y)

F.   (Colour the ducks with these words.)
     muffin ; drum ; puppet ; skunk ; thumb

32 Five Little Kittens

A.   1. first   2. lunch   3. basket
     4. five   5. cat
B.   1. D   2. A   3. B   4. I
     5. C   6. G   7. H   8. F
     9. J   10. E

33 Short Vowels (1)

B.   (Colour these pictures.)
     1.   2.   3.

D.   1. web   2. helmet   3. desk
     4. sled   5. lemon   6. well
     7. tent   8. penguin   9. net
    10. egg

34 Show and Tell

A.   1. white   2. two   3. water
     4. kitten(s) ; cat ; mouse
B.   Colour: red ; blue ; green ; white
     Number: five ; six ; two ; three
     Animal: cat ; pig ; mouse ; horse
     Drink: milk ; juice ; pop ; water

35 Short Vowels (2)

B.   (Circle these pictures.)

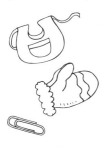

b	u	f	i	s	h	d
h	l	m	y	v	q	c
r	m	y	k	d	h	o
c	i	o	p	i	l	j
s	t	n	b	f	x	z
d	t	i	r	m	t	d
k	e	s	n	o	b	s
t	n	g	c	l	i	p
l	v	w	e	r	b	h

D.   1. d(o)g   2. t(o)p
     3. (o)ctopus   4. p(o)psicle
     5. f(o)rest

36 Favourite Recipes

A.   1. celery   2. cheese
     3. raisins   4. ants
B.   1. cracker   2. chocolate
     3. marshmallow 4. seconds

37 Short Vowels – Review

A.   Short "a" words: lamp ; plant ; cats
     Short "e" words: pen ; letter
     Short "i" words: kid ; window ; lizard
     Short "o" words: pot ; lollipop
     Short "u" words: mug ; butterfly

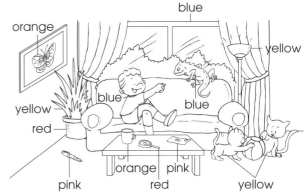

B.   1. bench   2. dart   3. witch
     4. card   5. bed   6. ship
     7. pan   8. block   9. jug
    10. clock   11. bottle   12. truck

38 Pancakes

A.   1. milk ; eggs ; flour ; butter
     2. batter   3. syrup
     4. plate
B.   1. pasta   2. candy
     3. Canada   4. spoon

39 Long Vowels (1)

A.   (Cross out these pictures.)
     1.   2.

     3.   4.

Answers

B. (Circle these words.)
1. find ; rhino
2. dinosaurs ; library
3. price ; high
4. pirates ; diamonds ; island
5. tiger ; spider ; sign

C. 1. snow   2. comb
3. bow   4. volcano
5. mango

D. (Colour these pictures.)

40 You Deserve A Break!

(Individual colouring of the circled differences and magnifying glasses)

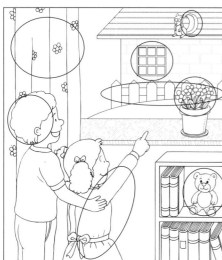

41 Wendy the Witch

A. (Individual colouring of the pumpkins)
1. sight ; night
2. blue ; too
3. hat ; bat

B. (Individual drawing)

42 Long Vowels (2)

A. 1. huge   2. hate
3. pine   4. rode
5. note   6. tube
7. dime

B. 1. cane ; C   2. glue ; B
3. bone ; A   4. snake ; J
5. phone ; H   6. bike ; I
7. slide ; F   8. rose ; E
9. whale ; G   10. cube ; D

43 Halloween Safety Rules

A. 1. light   2. trip
3. treat   4. rules

B. 1. clown   2. princess
3. witch   4. ghost

C. 1. candy   2. chips
3. lollipops   4. gum

44 Long Vowels – Review

A. 1. mule ; cute ; blue ; pupil
2. time ; dice ; wise ; pilot
3. cave ; blame ; basin ; tape
4. row ; joke ; stone ; post

B. 1. pipe ; C
2. mule ; A
3. cone ; E
4. tiles ; F
5. lake ; B
6. cake ; D

C. 1. s(u)s h i
2. w i n d(o)w
3. b(a)s e b a l l
4. a l l i g(a)t o r
5. p(i)n e a p p l e
6. h i p p(o)
7. t(u)l i p
8. h(i)g h w(a)y

6

45 Animal Homes

A. 1. wear   2. round
   3. sail   4. five
B. 1. E   2. B
   3. F   4. D
   5. G   6. A
   7. H   8. C

46 Nouns (1)

A. 1. house   2. kite
   3. bread   4. mitten
   5. rabbit   6. school
   7. cow   8. nurse
   9. glass
B. Person: mother ; driver ; nurse ; man
   Animal: cow ; beaver ; rabbit ; moose
   Place: house ; school ; beach ; park
   Thing: kite ; bread ; mitten ; jam
C. 1. boy ; kite
   2. girl ; apple
   3. dog ; table
   4. baby
   5. fish ; river
   6. cat ; milk

47 All Kinds of Homes

A. 1. Highrise
   2. Bungalow
   3. Two-storey house
   4. Houseboat
   5. Town house
   6. Trailer home
B. (Individual writing)

48 Nouns (2)

A. (Colour these words.)
   carrot ; star ; boat ; table ; water ; worker ; grass ;
   singer ; song ; bag
B. 1. ball   2. bike
   3. man   4. woman
   5. bird   6. tree
   7. dog   8. bench
   9. boy   10. girl
  11. kite   12. doll
C. (Individual writing)

49 The Man in the Moon

A. sky ; high ; moon ; soon
B. 1. fiddle
   2. moon
   3. spoon
   4. star
   5. sky

50 You Deserve A Break!

(Colour the flowers and vegetables with these words.)
beet ; feast ; field ; free ; green ; pea ; secret ; seed

51 Nouns (3)

A. Common Nouns:
   car ; butterfly ; school ; teacher ; mouse
   Proper Nouns:
   Rideau Canal ; Internet ; Halifax ; Kim ; Golden Retriever
B. 1. December ; Christmas
   2. September
   3. Saturday ; Sunday
   4. January ; New Year's Day
   5. Easter
   6. Tuesday
   7. May
   8. August

52 Planet Ex

A. 1. party
   2. playground
   3. planet
B. 1. apple ; pizza ; cake ; milk
   2. Tamagotchi ; football ; crayon ; computer
   3. socks ; jeans ; hat ; shirt

53 Nouns (4)

A. 1. flowers
   2. owl
   3. castle
   4. kids
   5. clown
   6. pets

B. (Suggested drawings)

1. mushrooms

2. bears

3. balloons

4. robots

5. stars

54 The Tooth Fairy

A. 1. girl
   2. tooth
   3. apple
   4. tooth
   5. mom
   6. box
   7. tooth
   8. box
   9. pillow
   10. fairy
   11. box
   12. fairy
   13. tooth

B. (Individual writing)

55 Nouns (5)

A. 1. sandwiches
   2. dishes
   3. watches
   4. boxes
   5. dresses
   6. glasses

B. 1. foxes
   2. switches
   3. addresses
   4. bushes
   5. buses
   6. benches

C. (Suggested drawings)

brushes   witches   octopuses

56 Dentist Dan

A. 1. dentist
   2. check-up
   3. toothpaste
   4. toothbrush
   5. brush

B. 1. sunglasses
   2. snowball
   3. pancake
   4. popcorn
   5. rainbow
   6. doorbell
   7. football
   8. butterfly

57 Sentences (1)

A. 1. ☹ 2. ☺
   3. ☹ 4. ☺
   5. ☹ 6. ☺
   7. ☺ 8. ☺
   9. ☺

B. 1. D   2. E   3. A
   4. B   5. C

C. 1. I like chewing gum.
   2. We buy gum in a candy shop.
   3. Bubble gum has many flavours.

58 Looking at Maps

A. (Individual drawing)

B. 1. Newtown
   2. Maple Street School
   3. Riverside Park
   4. Canada

59 Sentences (2)

A. 1. Grandpa ; Grandma
   2. bus
   3. Monkeys
   4. Nina
   5. duck
   6. Rome
   7. dog
   8. Summer
   9. Zeta ; Alice
   10. aliens

B. 1. E   2. A   3. D
   4. C   5. B

C. (Individual writing)

60 You Deserve A Break!

1. forehead
2. friend
3. hair
4. cheeks
5. wings
6. fairy
7. wand
8. window

61 Bird Watching with Grandpa

A. 1. blue jays
   2. cardinals
   3. robins
B. 1. mud
   2. grass
   3. twigs
C. 1. My grandpa lives in an apartment.
   2. We like to watch the birds.
   3. The eggs were a pretty colour.
   4. I used binoculars to see better.
D. 1. robin   2. nest
   3. trees   4. blue
   5. eggs   6. bird

62 Sentences (3)

A. 1. T   2. T   3.
   4.   5.   6.
   7. T   8.   9. T
   10. T
B. 1. They put on a very good play.
   2. They will go for a walk.
   3. Bruce is writing his journal.
   4. It snows in winter.
   5. Julia has a fluffy dog.
C. (Individual writing)

63 Canada Day

A. 1. July 1   2. red
   3. country   4. fireworks
B. 1. party   2. red
   3. sounds   4. colours
   5. flags
C. (Individual writing)

64 Sentences (4)

A. 1. ✗   2. ✔   3. ✗
   4. ✔   5. ✗   6. ✗
   7. ✔   8. ✔   9. ✔
B. 1. Do you go to that school?
   2. Can I have a candy?
   3. Is this your cap?
C. 1. Which cat do you like?
   2. Why couldn't you come to the party?
   3. Where did you go last Saturday?

4. Does your mother drive?
5. How did you do that?
6. Whose robot is this?
7. Are you sure you know the way?
8. When is Thanksgiving Day?
9. Who likes vanilla ice cream?

65 Family Picnic

A. 1. We went to the park on Canada Day.
   2. We get together to celebrate Canada Day.
B. 1. India   2. soccer
   3. pop   4. chicken
   5. fireworks

66 Sentences (5)

A. 1.   2. ✔   3.
   4.   5.   6. ✔
   7.   8.   9. ✔
   10. ✔
B. 1. How exciting!
   2. Oh dear!
   3. What a surprise!
   4. Watch your step!
C. (Individual writing)

67 Best Buddies

A. 1. Oliver ; Katie
   2. In Toronto
   3. "Goodnight Moon"
   4. They have a best buddy to play with.
B. 1. legs   2. arms
   3. eyes   4. socks
   5. boots   6. shoes

68 Punctuation and Capitalization

A. 1. .   2. !   3. .
   4. .   5. .   6. !
   7. ?   8. ?   9. !
   10. !   11. !
B. 1. Tyra named her dog Casey.
   2. The Gardners went to Italy for a holiday.
   3. Thanksgiving Day is in October.
   4. Ian lives on Scottfield Cresent.
   5. How did Jason get the key?
   6. Roald Dahl wrote "Charlie and the Chocolate Factory".

Answers

69 Robby Raccoon Finds a Friend

A. 1. D   2. A   3. C   4. B
B. 1. bird ; flew
   2. frog ; jump
   3. mouse ; ran
   4. Raccoon ; found

70 You Deserve A Break!

k	a	p	n	v	b	j	c	g	d
b	m	e	l	g	r	x	u	o	a
h	i	l	o	w	t	f		s	i
j	c	u	b	k	m	i	n	v	e
r	s	o	s	l	j	i	x	j	g
q	m		t	b	o	a	p	e	r
s	t	y	e	g	w	l	u	l	h
t	d	v	r	z	w	h	a	l	e
a	k	p	y	t	c	h	v	y	m
r	f	i	s	h	z	i	d	f	o
f	e	q	l	u	t	s		i	k
i	n	a	g	p	e	j	w	s	s
s	i	z	j	x	y	q	t	h	b
h	l	f	t		e	h	a	m	i
r	n	i	x	v	u	t	o	c	g
	b	h	k	v	s	h	a	r	k
	s	h	e	l	d	w	k	i	l

h	m	l	d	k	b	e	o	a	g
e	a	j	q	h	s	f	o	j	n
k	g	n	c	o	p		c	r	f
b	c	p	l	s	e	r	t	k	a
m	f	b	a	t	u	m	o	d	i
t	l	w	m	y	c	v	p	t	g
u	j	r	o	e	s	q	u	i	d
r	c	g	a	i	v	z	s	p	h
t	o	t	u	q	b	s	x	n	c
l	u	f		z	j	h	o	t	l
e	s	e	a	h	o	r	s	e	p
n	q	d	k	c	s	i	d	r	m
e	a	o	g	w	v	m	j		h
r	m		u	o	l	p	f	e	a
i	b	t	j	c	r	a	b	m	i
	h	s	d	s	g	k	r		c
	l	c	o	i		e	s		v

71 Word Order in Sentences

A. 1. The robbers stole the car.
   2. Jamie put the cat in the basket.
   3. The children are sitting at the table.
   4. Sharon turned on the computer.
   5. My sister goes to Westside School.
   6. Lester is drawing the curtains.
B. 1. The bird is in the sky.
   2. The boys are feeding the chicks.
   3. The boys have big baskets.
C. 1. Josh ate a big bowl of ice cream.
   2. They are skating at the rink.

72 My Dad Is the Best

A. 1. best ; west
   2. tight ; night
   3. play ; day
   4. ball ; mall
   5. cook ; book
   6. school ; cool
   7. glad ; dad
   (Individual writing of own rhyming words)
B. (Individual writing)

73 Pronouns

A. 1. she   2. it
   3. he   4. they
B. 1. They   2. She
   3. It   4. He
C. 1. I   2. We
   3. We   4. I
   5. I   6. I
   7. I   8. you

74 Hairy Harry

   1. present   2. cup
   3. red   4. black
   5. blue   6. planted
   7. grass   8. cup
   9. sun   10. water
  11. grow   12. like
  13. with   14. to
  15. hug   16. thank
  17. funny   18. present

75 Verbs (1)

A. 1. B   2. D   3. E
   4. G   5. F   6. A
   7. C

B. 1. goes   2. collect
   3. works   4. likes
   5. reads   6. give

C.

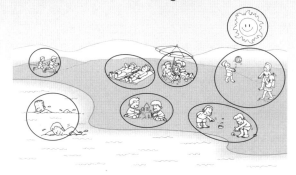

   1. play   2. swim
   3. shines   4. build
   5. pick   6. chat
   7. run   8. sunbathe

76 Animal Tails

A. 1. sail   2. now
   3. clap   4. pearl

B. 1. B   2. F   3. D
   4. A   5. E   6. C

C. (Individual answer)

77 Verbs (2)

A. 1. are   2. am
   3. is   4. is
   5. am

B. 1. is   2. am
   3. is   4. are
   5. is   6. are
   7. am   8. is

78 Beaver Tails

A. 1. Yes   2. No
   3. Yes   4. No
   5. Yes

B. 1. sweet   2. pastry
   3. winter   4. hot
   5. skate

79 Verbs (3)

A. 1. jumped   2.
   3. rained   4.
   5. tied   6.
   7. looked ; found   8.
   9. shared   10.
   11. rolled

B. 1. danced
   2. picked
   3. watched
   4. saved
   5. learned

C. 1. picked
   2. saved
   3. danced
   4. learned

80 You Deserve A Break!

(Colour the lily pads with these nouns.)
flower ; lilies ; grass ; water ; frog ; marsh ; kids ; bridge

81 Marvin the Magician

A. (Individual drawing)

B. 2 ; 1 ; 4 ; 3

82 Adjectives (1)

A. 1. sad girl
   2. cold drink
   3. beautiful butterfly
   4. stormy weather
   5. fast plane
   6. fat pig

B. 1. long   2. soft
   3. fierce   4. crispy
   5. slow   6. bright

C. (Individual answers)

83 If I Had a Magic Wand...

A. (Individual writing)

B. 1. aet ; eat
   2. fyl ; fly
   3. fere ; free
   4. snwo ; snow

C. 1. free   2. snow
   3. eat   4. fly

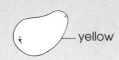

Answers

84 Adjectives (2)

A. 1. yellow (jelly bean)
2. (lollipops)
3. blue (kite)
4. (stars)
5. brown (teddy bear)
6. (apples)

B. 1. oval dish
2. a square mirror
3. a tiny bee
4. a huge bear
5. a round globe

85 Niagara Falls

A. 1. My family went to Niagara Falls.
2. The boat ride was exciting.
3. The fireworks display was amazing.

B. 3 ; 1 ; 4 ; 2

C. 1. Yes   2. No
3. Yes .   4. No

86 Prepositions

A. 1. beside   2. on
3. in   4. in
5. on   6. under
7. above   8. behind

B. (Individual drawing)

87 My Summer Vacation

A. 1. Stephen wrote about his summer vacation.
2. He wanted to visit Niagara Falls again.

B. 1. H   2. G   3. A
4. F   5. B   6. D
7. C   8. E

88 Articles

A. 1. the   2. an
3. a   4. a
5. an   6. the
7. a   8. the
9. an   10. the
11. an   12. a

B. 1. a penguin
2. the CN Tower
3. an elephant
4. the Canadian flag
5. an octopus
6. a hippo

C. 1. The ; the
2. The ; the
3. The ; an
4. a
5. The ; the

89 Synonyms and Antonyms

A. 1. glad   2. high
3. breezy   4. hop
5. dim

B. 1. (smile)   2. (frown)
3. (frown)   4. (smile)
5. (smile)

C. 1. cheap ; expensive
2. tall ; short
3. full ; hungry
4. cold ; hot
5. dirty ; clean
6. old ; young

90 You Deserve A Break!

Sydney's Answers:
black ; blonde ; blue ; brown ; purple ; red
Audrey's Answers:
frizzy ; giddy ; messy ; pretty ; puffy ; wobbly

12